THOSE

TWO

a novel

Those Two

Rheyn D. Maker

paperback edition
copyright 2022 Rheyn D. Maker
cover art by Tamark Books

PREFACE

I f there's anything worth telling, it's a good story. I'm not claiming this story's better than the billions of others that've already been told. But it needs telling all the same.

I'm not much for words. I just say it like I see it. Truth is, this story might be better if it were told by someone whose eloquence could articulate the morals and key points. The problem you're going to encounter is the storyteller: me.

So why doesn't someone else exonerate this tale?

Well, some stories belong to people, and those people have a right to it. Maybe it's connected to them, or maybe they witnessed it; maybe it's a story about them. I don't know the rules of fable ownership, exactly. Some people own stories like others own shoes and socks or a ball. It just belongs to them.

And this story is mine.

Don't be alarmed. It's not about me. I wouldn't bore you with my fantastic tales of going to and from school as a boy and, later, to and from work. My life isn't important enough to merit a retelling. Nope. This isn't a story about me; I own it for a different reason.

Unlike my life, their life stories deserves to be told. Someone ought to retell the events of their lives.

Why am I the one to expound on their history, you ask?

Because I'm their dad. I was there alongside them for a portion of the time. And what I didn't see in life, I watched closely in the hereafter. That's what I'm doing now. Watching and waiting.

Yep, no one knows those two better than me. I should be the one to tell their story.

That privilege is mine.

CHAPTER ONE

The seed tells us about the tree, and the tree tells us about the fruit. An apple seed yields an apple tree and an apple tree yields apples. Therefore, we can't really understand those two unless we know where they come from. Simple logic.

My section of the family tree is just like any other, nothing remarkable to make one branch stand out against the rest. But I tell you what, their mother was something else. Everything but normal. Not only was she one of the prettiest creatures with dark hair, brown eyes, and skinny legs to ever walk the southern corridor of the United States, but she also had an unmatched resolve to do what she wanted. Not just what she wanted to do, but also when she wanted to do it. And she usually did just that.

Arguably, this method of living can—and has—destroyed lives. Lesser people have tried to live by this standard, doing what you want when you want to do it. And it's no surprise that those people now reside in the cold and dark recesses of cell blocks or penitentiaries, their only company the echoing laments of their failed attempts at life. So when I say that Summer did what she wanted to do when she wanted to do it, I can see how you might get the wrong impression. Doing what you want, when you want, can be dangerous.

And I would agree with you. Normal people can't do that.

But Summer was not normal. I don't mean to imply that she hovered above the ground, talked to the dead, or shot electricity from her eyes. Not that kind of not normal. She just never wanted to do anything that wasn't right. It wasn't in her nature to do wrong. She was good, through and through. Tried and tested. No variance.

That kind of not normal.

We all have weak moments. Moments when we don't live up to our own ideals or expectations. Moments of weakness when we purposely do things we know we shouldn't.

Not her. Not Summer.

I've tried to recall when she looked evil in the face and welcomed it. There never was such a time. Evil looked her in the face and found no weakness, no crack or point of entry.

Occasionally, evil would muster its courage and make a mad charge to shatter her resolve. Alas, evil met the same result at every attempt—smashing like a pitiful wet wave on the strongest of cliff walls.

How she ended up with me, I'm not quite sure. I'm the luckiest son of a gun who every married up. Her resolve to stay with me, in spite of the many opportunities to move on, was nothing less than miraculous. Her story and mine are different altogether, but knowing the womb those two came from makes it easier to understand who they are.

Not that every womb produces the same likeness and character as the mother. To be sure, many a good woman has evacuated scum, and many a tramp has begotten angels. But in the case of Summer and her firstborn, the same goodness that existed in her passed on in perfect likeness. He was a biological product of the both of us, but he took all of her and none of me.

Toddrick came screaming into this world like any other child. An uncomfortable entrance to a cold and sterile room surrounded mostly by strangers, redeemed only by two people who shared the responsibility of bringing him into it. His dark hair and squished face didn't appeal to me. But Summer repeated over and over, "He's beautiful. He's beautiful."

I didn't think so. But I wasn't going to disagree with her, especially after the ordeal of childbirth.

After being released from the hospital, I looked at his tiny lump of a body resting in that plastic carseat. I wasn't much for driving over the speed limit anyway, but I drove home extra slow that day. I frequently checked on the little lump in the back seat, just to make sure he was there. I remember Summer laughed at me for it. I suppose taking such precautions wasn't my style.

Toddrick proved to be an easy baby. Not that I would've been the wiser if he was difficult. His mother did it all. Oh, I helped out here and there, but I just wasn't suited for watching a baby like Summer was. For starters, she wanted to be a full-time mom, and I didn't.

Once, when I was feeling fatherly, I offered to help. I could see that Summer needed rest. Long nights and broken sleep was written all over her face. I let her sleep in the bedroom, and I slept with the little fella on the couch. He rested his face down on my chest, and I couldn't help but appreciate the trust he had in me. He felt so warm against my shirt that I could have mistaken him for an oversized burning piece of coal. He melted into my body.

I awoke to the sound of a broken cry. My chest, which before was hot and occupied, was now rigid, cold, and vacant. Startled at his cry and subsequent disappearance from my view, I shot up from the couch. Summer was operating on some kind of sixth or seventh sense, an instinct that I hadn't yet cultivated. She darted out of the bedroom and scooped her arms down by the couch, lifting our crying son into her arms and cradling him to her breast.

She moved so quickly. I'd barely had a chance to sit upright.

I admit it. I dropped him.

Thankfully, Toddrick was forgiving. I had many chances to hold and cuddle him, despite my negligent breach of trust. Toddrick cried little and he fussed little. On the other hand, he played, smiled, and giggled all the time. If all babies were like Toddrick, more people would have children.

CHAPTER TWO

Little Jimmy, Summer's second-born, was not like his brother. He came into the world screaming just like Toddrick did—only it seemed to me like he never stopped.

Perpetual crying or no, that didn't deter his mother from loving him, from giving him thousands of little squeezes and kisses, or from doting on him. She acted like his crying was normal, like she wasn't bothered by it. Somehow, she was able to see past all the wailing and love that little one just as much as she loved Toddrick.

It was harder for me.

The consistent crying made it harder to appreciate Jimmy's presence. He screamed when he was eating, when he was bathing, when playing, and occasionally while he slept . . . if he ever slept at all. Lord knows I didn't.

I often thought there was a pouch of goodness inside Summer that was supposed to be shared with all her seed. On his way out, Toddrick burst it open and took most of the goodness. Jimmy, being second, may have received a few drops on his way out, but it was difficult to tell—at least for me.

I never dropped him on his head, like I did Toddrick, but he never gave me the chance, either. Jimmy didn't want to be held by me. I tried to coddle him, but he never allowed it. He would squirm and kick and push me away, crying the whole time.

Yet when I placed him in his mother's arms, he transformed into a different baby. He became quiet and calm. I guess I can't blame him for that. I would rather be in her arms too.

Toddrick was like his mom, and Jimmy was like his dad.

It's not that Jimmy was bad—definitely not. It was more like he was wild and not easily bridled. He wanted love and all good things that normal children want, but his path to get those things always seemed to be the hard way.

Consequently, he was a magnet for broken toys and personal injury. I can't remember a time when Jimmy's face didn't have a bruise or scratch on it, almost always self-induced. Accidents and crying children followed in his wake. If he wasn't hitting someone's child or taking someone's toy, he was most likely drawing on the walls, filling a sink with water, or dropping toys into the toilet.

Jimmy could change so suddenly. His anger and frustration shifted seamlessly to love and affection. At times, I saw him as a tiny Dr. Jekyll and Mr. Hyde. I didn't think Jimmy was a normal child.

In reality, it was just me. As I look back on it, I think he was the normal one and Toddrick was the anomaly.

Knowing that Jimmy and I got off on the wrong foot, I tried to strengthen the bond. He didn't readily accept my attempts to befriend him. Yet, he was playful—in a way that lasted too long or made me uncomfortable. His exuberance and energy extended beyond the time when everyone was done. I can recall scores of instances when I would tell the kids to stop jumping or stop throwing the ball or stop splashing in the water. All the kids would stop because I was the adult and, well—kids obey adults.

Kids besides Jimmy. Trying to rein him in after an exciting game was like trying to herd field mice with a net. Wasn't going to happen.

Jimmy rushed head-on in reckless energy. Consequences be damned.

CHAPTER THREE

Despite their differences in character, Jimmy loved Toddrick, and Toddrick loved Jimmy. In my mind, the polar opposites of their personalities made an impossible friendship. But there was something about Toddrick that Jimmy clung to. Something about Jimmy that, for Toddrick, made all the strangeness and high-stress manageable.

Perhaps for Jimmy, he got on well with Toddrick because he was so much like his mother. She was the only person who could comfort Jimmy as a baby. Jimmy clung to his mother, so I suppose it was reasonable that he would cling to the next best thing: someone with the same patient and loving disposition. Toddrick was, if nothing else, the male carbon-copy of his mother.

There was a symbiotic relationship between those two. Because they were around each other all the time, Toddrick and Jimmy had plenty of opportunities to observe each other's behavior. Toddrick got to see the consequences of disobedience. Jimmy was able to see the rewards of choosing the right. Jimmy learned how to act and Toddrick learned how not to act.

Those two became inseparable.

Toddrick wasn't perfect, and Jimmy wasn't all mistakes. Once, I spanked Toddrick. I can't remember why, but he cried like I'd punched him in the mouth. It was so rare an occasion when Toddrick got disciplined that the smallest tap induced tears.

Those two wanted to share everything. Jimmy was given a lollipop by one of his teachers at church. As I drove him home in the car, through the rear view mirror I saw him holding the candy in his hands. The wrapper was off, but he wasn't attacking it with the veracity that a child should.

I asked little Jimmy what the problem was. "Nothing," he responded. "I just want to share this with Toddrick." He held up the lollipop for me to see.

I wasn't sure how he envisioned sharing his candy with his brother until I saw the two standing in the kitchen trading licks on the sucker.

"Good grief," I exclaimed. "That's disgusting. Come on, guys. You don't have to share everything. Especially suckers."

Jimmy looked at me, a little crease appearing on his forehead. "Can I break a piece off for Toddrick?" his tiny voice asked.

"No," I said. "That's your sucker. No sharing suckers. Got it?" I made sure they both understood there were some things they couldn't, or shouldn't, share.

Another time the tables turned, and Toddrick had the treat. Another sucker. As far as I'm concerned, all suckers should be buried in a giant hole or trapped at the bottom of the sea. Stupid sticky cavity on a stick. Perhaps the sucker instances are more poignant to me because sharing them seems disgusting. Or maybe it's because I made rules barring there communal consumption.

Wanting to share his sucker and wanting to obey Daddy meant Toddrick had to be creative. I was watching, making sure they obeyed my "no sharing suckers" rule. "You can't lick the same thing," I declared. "You know the rule."

"It's okay, Dad," Toddrick said. "I've got a plan. I'll take a few licks, and then we can wash it. Then I'll let Jimmy take a few licks, and we can wash it again." He looked at me, the skin on his forehead forming a valley and his eyes wide, proud he'd found a way to comply with my rule and still get his brother a portion of the treat.

I admit, I was proud of their willingness to share, but I had to intercede for hygienic reasons. I broke the sucker with a rolling pin and gave the pieces to each.

Sure as day. Toddrick and Jimmy shared almost everything.

They played well together. True to his character, Toddrick always wanted to be the good guy, the hero, the savior. He couldn't stand being anything else. It wasn't in him to pretend to be the villain. All that was good was all Toddrick wanted to be.

Early one Saturday I watched the "Transformers" cartoon with them. It was frustrating to watch the "good guys" being portrayed as silly and reactive to the ploys of the "bad guys." It seemed to me that the good guys were less creative, less capable, and definitely less powerful.

Why it was necessary for me to make such a declaration in front of my sons' tender minds, I don't know. I shouldn't have said anything. After my declaration, "I'd rather be a Decepticon than an

Autobot," I looked at Toddrick, and his little brown eyes filled with innocent tears.

"What's the problem?" I asked, already knowing I'd hurt his feelings.

"It's just that . . ." He spoke slow, like he was trying to be cautious. Like he didn't want to say his thoughts because it might hurt my feelings. I'd heard that same tone a hundred times before, only from his mother. She was always trying to spare my feelings, and maybe Toddrick had picked up on that. "It's just that," he continued, "the Decepticons are bad, and the Autobots are good, and you said you like the Decepticons more. You aren't supposed to like the bad guys." Toddrick's resolve broke down, and the tears fell in unorganized torrents.

I cursed myself for being an idiot. I also cursed the idiotic people who made good seem weak in my children's cartoons. Why do the good guys always have to be so thoughtless or unmotivated? Give my children a strong hero who can think, who isn't afraid to destroy the villain. "I'm just joking," I said, eager to recover. "Optimus Prime is my favorite."

Toddrick smiled and wiped his eyes of wetness. "Really? Mine too."

His ability to forgive and forget was unparalleled.

As I said, in their moments of make-believe, Toddrick was always the good guy. That meant Jimmy had to be the bad guy. Jimmy accepted that. He loved to play with Toddrick more than he loved to be the good guy.

CHAPTER FOUR

Lightning storms in the south are impressive to behold. When I watched them from a distance, they made me feel small and powerless. Like I was an observer in a galactic battle taking place far away.

To a child, lightning is a phenomenon that induces awe, wonder, and fear. Its inexplicable power in the form of light. I can't remember how I felt about thunder and lightning as a child, but those two boys reverenced and respected it to the point of fearful shakes and screams.

I loved a good thunderstorm. They seemed to be nature's way of saying it could do something different if it wanted to—a break from the normal and the expected. Yet my perception of storms changed over time.

Summer and I would talk about their raw and natural power. The two of us would sit and watch the sky light up with purple and florescent white. Yet, after those two came along, well, let's just say there was many a night when I lost sleep due to storms.

The storms were never the problem. Sleep was lost

because those stormy nights were spent consoling those two little ones. They did not handle storms well.

Time after time I explained that lightning and thunder wouldn't hurt them. I tried to reason with those two. "During the last thunderstorm, did either of you get hurt?" Silently, they shook their heads. "No. Of course not. It didn't hurt you last time, what makes you think it will hurt you this time?" I hoped to prove that because nothing happened last time, nothing would happen this time, and that in the future, nothing was going to harm them then, either. I know it's not the best motto to live by, and it definitely isn't a principle applicable against all life's problems, but I was desperate to get some sleep.

Flawed principle or no, it didn't work. Reasoning never worked. They were perpetually scared of the storms.

Once again, on a separate night's cannonade of thunder, their terrified cries roused me from sleep. I knelt next to their beds. Their eyes were wide with terror. I held their little hands. "Do you guys know anyone who's been hit by lightning?"

They shook their heads, eyes still wide. The sky ignited with brilliant light, and their bodies trembled beneath the blankets. "If I knew anyone who was hit by lightning, they would be dead," Jimmy said in his small and frightened voice.

I tried not to smile at his dramatic proclamation. "If nobody you know has been struck by lightning, that's a pretty big indicator that *you* won't be hit by lightning. It hasn't hit anybody you know, so it's not going to hit you. There is nothing to be afraid of." Again, I knew this was flawed logic. Sleep—all in the name of sleep. I'm a simple-minded man, but I hoped it would work.

It didn't.

I tried to illustrate that hardly anyone in the world's been struck by lightning. The ratio of those struck to those not struck was such a minute percentage that the probability of it happening to them was infinitely small. "It's almost impossible for you to be hit by lightning." They were toddlers, not scientists or mathematicians.

Again, they didn't get it.

So I did what any sleep-deprived parent would do. I started making things up. Lightning is God sneezing and thunder is when He laughs, to which Toddrick replied, "I don't like it when God gets a cold."

During one storm I told them I'd ordered thunder and lightning for their mother as a gift, like when you order flowers. Only the lightning storm was a lot more expensive. "I feel bad that I ordered the storm now," I said. "I didn't want to make you scared, but it's for Momma. You don't want me to cancel her gift, do you?" I looked at them with my best version of puppy dog eyes. Sleepy puppy dog eyes.

I could see the conflict working through their minds. They hated the storm, but loved it when their mother got nice things. I was going to succeed in switching their fear to acceptance. I was on the verge of congratulating myself for future nights of uninterrupted sleep.

"Daddy."

Jimmy's frightened voice was muted by his blanket, which he had over his head. Even though it was a warm summer's night, both he and Toddrick were securely tucked away under all their bedding. The trembling in his voice aroused my sympathies, but only a little. I was beyond ready to go back to sleep.

"Yes?" I forced patience into my voice.

"I won't whine if I can sleep in Toddrick's bed."

I saw the opportunity and capitalized on it. "If you promise not to scream or cry at the lightning anymore, you can sleep on his bed every night there's a storm." I could feel my own eyes widen with excitement. "Does that sound good?"

"Okay, Daddy," he said as he crawled off his bunk. In one hand he was carrying a little yellow truck, and in the other hand his favorite blue blanket. "I'm still going to be scared, but I won't scream no more."

His honesty was touching. I wondered how I could get so mad at such a little fella, and then five minutes later be so pleased with him. I guess that's part of being a dad . . . the part I'm not proud of. I could go from happy to angry as fast as a race car goes from zero to sixty. Like I said, we all have a little bit of Dr. Jekyll and Mr. Hyde in us.

I'm sure every parent experiences what I have. At times, your children bring you such joy. Other times you try not to get embarrassed that they belong to you. And there are those rare times when you just watch for the sake of watching—a moment when you view your children as individual human beings. Not as your responsibility, not as persons you have to mold or train in a certain way. Just as people trying to be people.

Those were the best times for me. I learned more about their true character that way.

What's ironic is that they did just fine without my hovering over them. Makes me wonder if I put too much effort into trying to make them act a certain way. Maybe they could have done with a few less scoldings and a little more encouragement from their dad.

Children are a strange and controversial topic. They are all supposed to be innocent and protected or adored or whatever. But I don't like other people's children. And really, I don't like other children's parents. It's my opinion that too many kids are rotten, and too many parents think their kids are angels.

It may be heresy, but there isn't any better place to observe this dichotomy than at church. People try to be perfect while judging others because they're not perfect. Church ought not to be what it is sometimes.

Nonetheless, we were church folk. Toddrick was an example of a perfectly behaved child. Everyone loved him. It was common for a teacher or parent to come to me and say how wonderful Toddrick was. Even the bad kids knew he was good. They didn't seem to understand him, so they left him alone. There was a certain coolness about him that helped shield him from harassment and bullies. He was operating on a level of his own and never got involved in mischief. He listened; he was quiet and knew the answers. He reacted right all the time.

Jimmy, on the other hand, developed a reputation as a hell-raiser, and he did so in record time. He wasn't intentionally disruptive, and he never destroyed *crucial* property, but his tunnel vision made it impossible to see the immediate effects of his actions.

He was smarter and more coordinated than other four-year-olds in his class. All that energy and intelligence bursting out of such a little fella is hard to contain. Whenever he saw Toddrick, whether it was in passing in the hallway or when he was singing with a group, he wouldn't sit still until he got near his brother. Didn't matter where or when, Jimmy was going to get Toddrick's attention.

Once a year the primary Sunday School would host a program where each child would stand at the podium and speak to the congregation. Often times, church services seemed mundane or absent of significant power. But when I heard simple things said by simple little people, it made me feel lighter than my normal heavy disposition. I imagine all parents feel the same. From the mouths of babes, right? Those moments when our children spoke from the pulpit were some of the greatest times for me at church.

I was both a proud man and a proud father. I esteemed my children as intelligent, and I wasn't going to let a public appearance ruin that. I'd seen it a hundred times. Children get in front of a crowd and hem or haw about something that nobody understands because nobody can hear what the kid is saying. Or maybe the kid just has no idea what he or she is saying.

Wouldn't happen to my child. If they were in front of a microphone, they knew what to say.

Therefore, in preparation, I made sure Toddrick and Jimmy knew their parts backward and forward. I practiced with them, went over it again and again. They memorized their small discourses, word for word and line for line. I suppose that, ideally, you'd like them to say things from the heart rather than just rote memorization. But we fill their minds with what we can and hope some of it sticks.

Our congregation was big and boasted a primary of over a hundred children. On this special child-focused Sabbath, most little ones took their turn at the podium and struggled through their lines. I know it shouldn't matter whether or not they struggled through what they had to say. They're just kids. Furthermore, it's not *how* it's said, it's *what* is said. Besides, public speaking is terrifying for most adults. Why should I be annoyed that little ones get up and have a hard time?

I sat in the middle of the chapel, a strategic place from where I could see both Jimmy and Toddrick. I'd been trained to always keep an eye on Jimmy, so it was normal that I would position myself where I could focus on him and still see everything else. As I looked at the kids up there, I couldn't help but wonder if children's actions were a reflection of the way their parents prepared them. If the child had no direction or didn't know what to say, was it because mom and dad didn't do their job right?

Some kids were shy, and others had teachers whisper the words in their ears. For those that could read, notes or papers were employed to refresh memories. A few kids got up and giggled until a teacher led them away from the microphone.

Of my two, Jimmy was the first to take the podium. For a moment I thought he was gonna be a giggler. But after he smiled real big, he aimed his tiny discourse at the congregation. "I can show reverence by controlling my feet and by not running and not kicking other people." It was a great run-on sentence. He spoke in a voice that was sincere, like it was a promise of future behavior. I'm sure that whichever teacher helped Jimmy choose what to say had probably experienced a few problematic moments caused by little Jimmy's feet.

Having said his piece, Jimmy sat back in his chair.

I didn't try to disguise the relief I felt when Jimmy was no longer the focal point of the congregation. His turn was surprisingly fantastic! No one got hurt and nothing broke. You may think me unfatherly for expecting such occurrences from my little Jimmy, but I'd been trained to expect them. Disaster was the common trend with him. I felt the tension leave my neck and shoulders when he was safely tucked away with his class.

Several minutes later, Toddrick got up. Unlike Jimmy's brief statement, Toddrick had a few sentences to recite. Having gone over the part with him, I knew it was long. I thought for sure he'd forget it.

At the podium, Toddrick started talking. His voice filled the chapel, and Jimmy's head perked upward. I saw it pop above the rest of the little heads like a ground hog looking for the sun. He must have recognized his brother's voice. I was trying to watch Toddrick, but Jimmy stood on his chair and started waving his hands over his head. Jimmy shouted, "That's my brother! Toddrick! Hey, Toddrick!" The nearest teacher tried to calm Jimmy and make him sit down, but the little guy was intent on getting his brother's attention.

The congregation chuckled. I heard someone say, "That's cute," and someone behind me said, "He sure likes attention."

Well, Jimmy didn't care one lick about the smiles and laughs he was getting from the audience. His only objective was to get Toddrick to acknowledge him.

Now I had prepared my boys to say their parts, but I never rehearsed what to do if you brother goes crazy during your presentation. Toddrick, always better than I estimated, stopped talking into the microphone and waited for the crowd to stop giggling. He turned around and waved to his brother. "Hi, Jimmy." His voice cool and even, genuine, without admonition or unkindness, like he wasn't inconvenienced at all.

Having established contact with Toddrick, Jimmy smiled with satisfaction and sat down. Toddrick cleared his throat and continued from where he'd left off, never skipping a beat, never missing a word.

I can't remember exactly what he said, something about obedience and trusting in doing the right thing. What I *do* remember is how that public, yet private, interaction made me feel.

I learn from my children all the time. But this day I learned an especially poignant lesson. There were hundreds of times when those two came to me wanting to play, but I was busy working—doing something I thought was important. After watching Toddrick interact with Jimmy, stopping like that just to say hi, I questioned where my priorities were. I felt like maybe I'd put too much emphasis on things that weren't urgent, even though I thought they were. Work is always going to be there and it has to get done. But why couldn't I spare more time for those two little ones?

Just because you're doing something important doesn't mean you can't stop for three seconds and say hello to the people you love. And if someone you love is doing something important, don't be afraid to make a ruckus to get their attention.

Those two taught me that.

CHAPTER FIVE

I t made sense to have them in the same sport simultaneously. Toddrick tried a season of soccer, so Jimmy did too. Usually it could be arranged to have them play on the same team. Their birthdays were separated by eleven months, so for one month of a year they were the same age. That helped in advocating playing together.

Despite being close in age, Jimmy and Toddrick had very different body types and statures. Toddrick was taller and skinny with dark brown hair. Jimmy, on the other hand, was more compact, shorter but stronger, his hair golden against his light skin. Jimmy wanted to keep up with Toddrick, so he had to work harder for his little legs to cover as much distance.

So, as Jimmy continually exerted himself, his tiny muscles grew strong and tenuous. He became a downright good athlete. Not because he was athletic. Not at all. Rather, he was a good athlete because he learned to break those mental barriers that hold most of us back. Pain tells are bodies to stop. From what I could see,

Jimmy learned to ignore the pain at an early age. And I dare say that Jimmy could have out played everyone at anything . . . if he'd also developed respect for the rules and coaches.

As it was, Jimmy never seemed to get the concept of teams or sports in general. He ignored the rules and those who tried to coach him. It was bittersweet to watch. One minute I was as pleased as could be that he was trying so hard, but the next I would be looking for a place to hide because he'd run amuck of the game, causing all types of mayhem. It was clear that he was faster and more agile than most kids, but he never tried to play the game.

He'd kick the ball off the field or pick it up with his hands, all things he knew he wasn't supposed to do. He thought it was funny to go outside the boundaries or lead the game in a direction outside of normal play.

That's' one of my favorite things about athletics. Sports can teach obedience without actually teaching obedience. There are rules that must be complied with in order for the game to proceed. Just like in sports, life has rules that must be complied with, or else it's difficult to proceed.

Jimmy didn't have any regard for rules, for whatever game he played. As I watched him run everywhere, I hoped it wasn't a foreshadowing of future noncompliance.

Sometimes I was embarrassed by Jimmy's behavior. Nonetheless, I made it a point to be at his games as often as I could.

There were times I was just plain mad at the boy for not doing what he was supposed to do. And sometimes I was ashamed of my feelings. I always thought parents should feel good about their children's performance and be their encouragement. I beamed with pride every time Toddrick took to the field. Unfortunately, I wasn't the best cheerleader for my little Jimmy. But when I heard a few parents refer to him as the "stupid boy" who didn't know the rules, something clicked inside my mind, and I had an immediate change in perspective.

I didn't like how he didn't conform, but I certainly wouldn't talk negatively about my own son, and I most definitely wouldn't talk about someone else's child in such a demeaning way. At least out loud. I wondered why Jimmy didn't simply follow the crowd, take the easy road—stay between the lines. He did his own thing and suffered for it.

But no father likes to hear his child called stupid. Hearing someone else say it made me realize how ridiculous I was—trying to force him to act a certain way. I was the stupid one for putting him in an environment that would expose one of his greatest weaknesses.

That day, I felt smaller and less manly, less fatherly and less decent, than I'd ever felt. I was crushed and disappointed with myself. Crushed for Jimmy. The realization that I could be so hard on my own flesh and blood nearly broke me. Who was I, and who were they, to judge a six year old?

I changed my approach. Day after day I talked to him, encouraged him to play by the rules, stay within the lines. I recall his little child face, trying to show resolve. His eyes, fiery and brown, are permanently etched in my mind.

The more I got down on his level and talked to him, eye to eye, the stronger the connection I felt. I don't know why I didn't see it before, but he had so much untapped potential in him, so much determination. There was something strong behind those eyes. Will-power.

Jimmy came around. He gained the respect of his peers and their parents. He was a good athlete, especially for a child. He played at a level beyond his age, and his energy was unmatched.

True to form, Toddrick excelled. He was limber, attentive, and unlike Jimmy, naturally athletic. The same obedience that he demonstrated at home, he exhibited with his coaches. He caught on fast and learned the concept of the games. He was a respecter of lines and boundaries.

Those two played everything together. When Toddrick played baseball, Jimmy played too. They tried karate, tennis, and wrestling. As always, little Jimmy tried to perform at Toddrick's level. I appreciated the brotherly sportsmanship that existed between them. They sparred together, played catch, and ran together.

When I was a kid, I played with my brothers too. I reckon most kids who play together develop a bond, just like me and my brothers did. But as I watched Jimmy and Toddrick, I thought there might be something different there. Maybe something special.

Even so, I didn't understand the strength of their relationship until one summer morning.

Those two both auditioned for the city's junior swim team. The requirements were simple: swim two laps of the pool. During tryouts, Toddrick swam the laps with ease. Jimmy, however, struggled the entire way. I thought I was going to have to jump in and save him a few times, but he made it.

Mrs. Robinson, the swim coach, told me Jimmy wasn't going to make the cut. "He'll probably be ready next year, but not now. He doesn't have the arm strength," she said.

And she was right. He wasn't a strong swimmer. She wasn't going to get any complaints from me.

Imagine my surprise when the roster was published and Jimmy's name was on it—right underneath Toddrick's.

"I thought Jimmy wasn't going to make the team," I said, cornering Coach Robinson by the edge of the pool. "What happened?"

She shrugged her shoulders and smiled. "I don't know. It just seems wrong to let Toddrick swim and not Jimmy. Little Jimmy tried his hardest, and he did make it across the pool." She broke eye contact with me. Maybe it was because she saw the mortification in my eyes. I felt like Coach Robinson had broken an unspoken promise. Could she see that too? "I don't have any other six year olds that can do that, swim the entire length of the pool." She looked at me again. "It wasn't good." She looked like she was considering something, like maybe she might change her mind. "But he made it." Her smile widened. "I'm sure I'll regret it later."

At their first swim meet, the crowd was packed tight against the edges of the pool. It wasn't a big competition; just a bunch of little kids treading water. But I could tell that some considered this a serious event. Parents, mostly. I'm sure they believed their little swimmers were the next generation's aquatic athletes.

I suffered from no such delusions. Toddrick and Jimmy were not future Olympians. However, I was happy to have proof that, if left in water, my children would not drown. Knowing they could swim on their own was a small but significant comfort in a world fraught with countless ways to accidentally die.

There were too many people for me to see the pool without pushing through the crowds. I didn't want to be obnoxious, so I lingered near the back and looked for cracks in the heads of bystanders. I was pleased when Coach Robinson slapped a clipboard against my stomach.

"Here," she said. "I need a line judge." She pointed toward the edge of the pool. "Go sit in one of those chairs and write down which lane is the winner."

I was more than willing to oblige. I stepped through the crowds and got complete visual access to the pool.

Toddrick's age group was the first to swim. He did as I expected he would. He finished second in his heat behind a ten-year-old. Not too shabby for a first timer. Because of his ability to listen and learn, he progressed quickly. After doing something once or twice, he could do it so well that it was like he had been doing it all his life. He was that way with most things—including swimming.

I heard Jimmy's name called over the loud speaker. The amplified voice directed him toward lane two. Jimmy's normal demeanor was energetic and bold, but as he walked to the edge of the pool, he displayed a very different attitude. He was timid and looked pensive— very unsure. The image of a little boy frightened of lightning flashed through my mind. This was rare. He was scared.

The swimmers took their places. I was the timer of lane four, so I was close enough to see little Jimmy in lane two. He still looked uncomfortable as he positioned himself near the water's edge. Looking at the line of boys, it was clear that Jimmy was the smallest in height by at least a foot.

"Swimmers ready!" the moderator yelled. No one objected, so the whistle sounded loud and sharp.

The swimmers dove head first in the water and started swimming toward their goal. I looked in Jimmy's lane and realized he wasn't in the water. After a few seconds, he jumped in feet first and began to swim. Halfway down the length of the pool, he began to slow. The rest of the boys had already finished and were exiting the pool. My heart sank as I watched Jimmy struggle. His wide and frightened eyes were inches above the water, and his arms frantically pulled him toward the lane dividers. At least there was no danger. He could hold on to the buoys until I could jump in and retrieve him.

Despite how the crowd urged him onward, Jimmy refused to let go of the lane dividers. I pulled off my shirt in preparation to jump in and help him finish the race. Just as I was about to enter the water, I heard a splash.

A small body was swimming under the water like a frog in Jimmy's direction. At first, I thought it was a lifeguard or one of the coaches. Coach Robinson stepped next to me and put a hand on my shoulder.

"It's Toddrick," she said.

I jogged to the side of the pool that put me closest to Jimmy. A few feet away from him, the swimmer in the water surfaced. I smiled at the dark hair and dark eyes. It *was* Toddrick.

It was hard to make eye contact with Jimmy. His eyes were so large and unfocused. I shouted his name and waved my hands, trying to get his attention. By the time he looked at me, Toddrick was only a few feet away.

"Are you okay, little guy?" I shouted above the pool ambiance.

"I'm scared, Dad." His eyes darted from side to side like he was looking for an escape. "I need help." His lip quivered while he spoke.

Before I could say anything else, Toddrick tapped him on the shoulder. "Jimmy."

Jimmy turned to face his brother. He didn't let go of the buoy, but his eyes were no longer frantic. They were no longer searching for an escape.

"Do you want to swim with me?" Toddrick asked.

"I'm a little scared."

"I'll be with you the entire way," Toddrick said while treading water. "Look." He motioned to the end of Jimmy's lane. "It's just over there. I'm with you."

Jimmy's resolve restored itself, and he pushed off the buoy and started paddling through the water. Toddrick matched Jimmy stroke for stroke. The crowd cheered for Jimmy as if he was the greatest swimmer in the world, finishing the greatest race in the history of mankind. Jimmy put his hands on the ledge and lifted himself out of the pool, and the crowd's applause erupted like a volcano.

I'd like to say that I had a good effect on my children, that I could get their obedience because they loved and respected me. I consider myself one of their chief motivators in life. But if I said I had as much influence on Jimmy as Toddrick did, that would be a lie.

That day at the pool, I was going to do the fatherly thing and jump in the water and take Jimmy out of danger. I suppose anyone could have done that. Only Toddrick could have gotten Jimmy to swim the rest of the way.

This act, observed by a crowed of a hundred people, affected me so much that it was impossible to see Toddrick or Jimmy the same way again. It was almost like I wasn't needed for anything in their life besides providing a roof over their heads and food on their table. The bond growing between those two was stronger than I had thought possible.

I observed the crowd when the boys emerged from the pool, and for those that understood the act of brotherly kindness, they too recognized the power of what transpired. There was hardly a dry eye among those of us who witnessed it.

CHAPTER SIX

All parents think their kids are special. I've heard many a parent talk about how beautiful or how talented their child is. But from my perspective, their child was neither beautiful nor talented. It's a parent's weakness. We see the good and the potential in our children and think everyone else sees it too. It's not just that we think our children are capable or have potential, it's that we think our children are more capable and have more potential than other children.

Knowing this is common, I've come to accept that my kids are special to me . . . and only to me. I try to be levelheaded about their abilities and not suffer from the delusion that my children are better or more capable than other children.

I've only had the chance to observe those two, but I assume their experiences and feelings are not unique to them, though they are deeply personal. I would say it's not uncommon for siblings to grow up feeling close to each other.

When it came to Toddrick and Jimmy, they were

forced to spend time together. Their beds were in the same room, so they slept at the same time. They woke up together, ate meals at the same table, waited at the same bus stop, sat next to each other on the bus and road home from school together. There was hardly a time in their youth when one brother was without the other.

They attended Boy Scouts in the same building. On the weekends they watched the same TV shows and played the same video games. The night time and morning routine had them brushing their teeth together, sharing the same tube of toothpaste and praying at the same time.

Summer read to them every night, which might seem insignificant, but when people hear the same words, it can create a similarity in mental patterns. At least I think so.

Toddrick and Jimmy were doing the exact same things almost every day from the time they were born to the time they entered grade school. Even though their personalities were drastically different, they slept, woke, and lived in the same world, only feet away from each other.

Try living that closely with someone and not knowing them.

Toddrick and Jimmy exited childhood and entered adolescence. For the most part, their characters were set. Their likes, dislikes, and personal preferences were becoming more and more distinct.

Grade school is awkward for everyone, unless one is unaware of their own awkwardness. Then it's just awkward for everyone else. Pre-pubescent bodies are changing, and emotions and hormones are fluctuating.

If ever there was a time period that could disappear without anyone caring, it was the years between the fifth and eighth grades.

Boys and girls growing, but not proportionately to the sizes of their heads. Ears, noses, eyes and mouths all arranged asymmetrically. Torsos with bony limbs gangling about, sprouting out like beans on crooked stocks.

Most go through it. There are a few lucky ones who look proportionate through all stages of life. Toddrick was one those.

But alas, nothing skipped Jimmy. No grace would save him from the woes of life. He was spared no trial. Jimmy was the last of his age to grow, and the first to run headlong into the limelight in his awkward stages. On multiple occasions, Toddrick defended Jimmy from childish jeers and embarrassing outcomes.

As much as he tried, Toddrick couldn't save Jimmy from himself.

CHAPTER SEVEN

It's never easy to discuss the birds and bees with your children. In fact, we call it the birds and the bees to disguise the fact that we are talking about sex. That fact alone is evident it's not easy to talk about. I don't know why it's hard to discuss, but it is. Sex. One of the most natural, one of the most important things in life, and we gloss over. Ignore it until it stares us in the face.

As I see it, my kids can either learn about sex from a teacher, through their own experience, or I can tell them about it. I'd rather teach it to my children the way I want it to be taught.

Not only is sex a painful conversational topic, but knowing *when* to have the talk and *how* to have it are problematic. It's like a triple threat: the topic itself, when, and how. I didn't want to do it too soon and mess up their minds, but I didn't want to wait until it was too late, lest they figure it out on their own. I knew I couldn't control them, but I wanted to prepare them. Educate them, at least.

Movies and television shows contribute to the discussion a little too much and in the wrong ways. Furthermore, the music of this generation is like one long and exaggerated sex education course. It's no wonder we struggle with sexual harassment and an abundance of out-of-wedlock children.

I knew I had to do something with those two boys.

Far sooner than I expected, a situation forced my hand.

Occasionally our little family ventured out into the wilderness to enjoy Mother Nature. Call them vacations if you will, though they never felt like a true vacation. It was more like trying to prove I could do without modern conveniences for a few days. I was always eager to get home after a few nights of sleeping on the ground.

On one such night while we camped under the stars, I overheard a conversation between Toddrick and Jimmy. Voices carry in the silence of night, and they must have thought mom and dad were sleeping.

"I've got a girlfriend."

I recognized Jimmy's mousy voice. It was a pretty bold announcement for a fourth grader.

"You do not," Toddrick replied, his tone dripping with doubt. "You're not even old enough."

"Do too have one. And you can have one whenever you want. Age doesn't matter. It's not like there's rules."

Typcial Jimmy attitude. But something rubbed me wrong about what he'd said. Inwardly I berated myself for not thinking about it earlier. Jimmy had a point. I hadn't established rules. Poor parenting on my part.

"Who is it, then?" Toddrick still sounded disbelieving, but I could hear genuine curiosity in his voice. "And don't make up a name. I know everyone you know. *And*

I'll see her on the bus or at school. I'll know if you're lying."

Perhaps the shock in his voice came from the fact that despite all his talents and popularity, he didn't have a girlfriend himself. As if a part of him were saying if he couldn't have one, Jimmy couldn't either. Jealousy. Rare for Toddrick.

"Nivea Thompson," Jimmy blurted out her name and laughed. "She's my girlfriend. And Susan Woodard too. And I'm not too young. I just don't know what you're supposed to do with them." His voice changed from jovial to thoughtful. "With girlfriends, I mean. I guess they're kind of boring."

"You're not *supposed* to do anything." Toddrick sounded exasperated, but then his voice took on a quizzical tone like Jimmy's. Like he was curious. "I guess you just look at them?"

"Look at them. Why?" Jimmy's question was sincere. "Brett Breckenridge said he touched one, once."

"Touched what?"

"A girl."

"He did not. You and Brett don't know anything about girls. Mom and I have talked and I know what you're supposed to do with a girl, but not till you're married. Mom said it's the best thing, to be married and in love with someone." He paused. "But I still don't know what to do with a girlfriend."

Bless my sweet Summer. I may not have had the sense to talk to my oldest in time, but my perfect wife did.

"Do you think Dad touches Mom?"

My heart rate increased and I looked at Summer. She was sleeping soundly right next to me.

Toddrick gasped. "I don't know, and I don't want to

talk about it."

"Why? I think I saw him do it once."

"Do what?" Toddrick was annoyed.

"Touch Mom, dummy."

"Of course he touches Mom. They hold hands and kiss all the time. That isn't a secret!" Toddrick's tone had a hint of finality, like he was trying to say the conversation was over.

There was silence for a few minutes before Jimmy continued. "I know, but," he hesitated. "This touching was different. they were—"

Toddrick blew air out is mouth. "Jimmy, that kind of touching leads to babies. It's none of our business."

I was mortified but had to stop myself from laughing.

"Babies?" Jimmy mocked.

"Yep. Mom also said if you do things at the wrong time, it can mess you up real good. Destroy your head, kind of. Your heart, too. You can get sick like you have the flu, only it lasts for a long time and medicine won't help."

"Well." Jimmy's tone was full of accusation. "Well, no one told me anything about girlfriends, so I'm gonna ask Nivea what she wants to do."

"I'm telling you now," Toddrick said. "You're not supposed to do anything."

I laughed to myself, but at the same time I felt like I'd done my sons a disservice. How could they not know? I had to get more involved in their lives.

The next day as we were throwing our fishing lines into the creek, I had the "birds and the bees" talk with my fourth- and fifth-grade sons. I'm not gonna tell you what I told them, because I know you'll think I did it all wrong. But by the time Jimmy had caught his first fish, he knew what to do with his girlfriend—nothing. He also knew what to do with his wife—everything.

Now I didn't expect those two to be prudes, but I did expect them to be filled with virtue. Ain't anything wrong with kissing. I encourage it. But the closer you get to the fire, the more you start smelling like smoke and the bigger chance you're gonna get burned. Doesn't matter who you are.

I worried about Jimmy. I was uncomfortable just hearing him talk about it. He was excited, curious, and explorative. He rushed into things, consequences be damned. For some things like sports or playing with his brother, that could be all right. But when it comes to love and sex, the wrong choice could alter a person's outlook on life forever. For some ill choices, it seems there's no recovery.

But I knew I couldn't make him do the right thing. He was going to do what he wanted to. He was a stallion that could only be broken by life. His way or no way at all.

And I'd already decided that when life broke him, I was going be there to pick up the pieces.

Choices can change the trajectory of a life. You can destroy your own life through bad choices, and then other people can destroy your life with bad choices too. Double whammy.

I didn't worry about Toddrick as much, at least when it came to sex. He seemed to approach the topic with enough reverence and respect to abate any concerns. Toddrick seemed to get the heavy things. He trusted counsel.

I'm a man, but once I was a boy. I know how keenly a young man's heart can feel. They say females love the strongest, but I don't think that's true. Men get love sick, just like women. Just because a man doesn't read a romance novel or bask in the popularity of the latest chick flick doesn't mean that he loves any less.

I'd been watching Toddrick, and I knew the telltale signs of admiration. He was starting to be sweet on Lisa Betford. As sweet as a ten-year-old could be, anyway. I wished I'd had the same sense when I was a boy. He would sneak a few glances here and there, quietly watching her when he thought no one was looking.

He took every chance to open the door for her and pick up things she dropped. At social functions, he'd bring her a cookie or a cupcake. He did small things to show he cared, without flash or drawing attention to himself or her.

Little Lisa was a sweet girl and came from good, educated people. My fear for Toddrick was rejection. Her family was well to-do and had the finer things of life, and that in great abundance. We weren't poor by any stretch, but we weren't rich like the Betfords were.

My fears that he'd be alone in his admiration were unwarranted. It didn't take long before she returned his actions with innocent, shy smiles and an occasional reddening of the face.

If good behavior in young people could yield perfect companionship, I would say Lisa and Toddrick made a good fit. Both were smart, intelligent, and well-behaved. But feelings shared among youth can't always be preserved. Admiration passes from person to person over the course of our developing years. People and feelings change. It's rare that childhood fancies blossom into lasting relationships.

Still, I couldn't help it. Deep down inside, I smiled at

the potential match. Something told me that I'd get to see more of little Lisa later in life.

CHAPTER EIGHT

was wrong.

I wasn't going to see more of Lisa, or anyone else.

At least not on earth.

I never accounted for what could go wrong in life.

Life is blind to who needs what and who already has what. It can compound hardships for one individual, but on the other hand it can bestow gift after gift to another. Life doesn't ascribe to status quo.

And so it was with me. On a routine visit with my doctor, it was discovered that I had terminal cancer. I was going to die. Soon.

I'd thought I'd spent enough time with my sweetheart and those two. When death wasn't staring me in the face, I had all the time in the world. But when I learned I *didn't* have all the time in the world, my feelings changed. In life, I did not balance my time or energy correctly.

My last six months moved incredibly fast. I was like a man trying to hold life in a bucket with a hole in the bottom. I tried to be positive through the ordeal. I made an effort to enjoy the *taste* of food, instead of just putting so much of it in my mouth. I tried to enjoy the sunrise and the sunset instead of using them as symbols to mark the progression of days.

This isn't my story. It's the story of those two boys. But if I didn't say that I'd made a mistake in not enjoying them properly, I'd be remiss in sharing a valuable lesson. I never fully appreciated the time I had until I had no time.

I regretted every time I got angry, and I got angry a lot. I regretted every time I said something unkind to those two. I thought I had done well, but when I knew I wasn't going to see them anymore, I questioned everything I'd ever done.

Unbeknownst to almost everyone on the planet, I slipped out of this life.

Those two lost a father.

It's common enough. People die every day. Compensating for the loss of a father is impossible. The time that might have been, the example that could have been set. Children need fathers just as much as they need mothers.

My death activated a generous life insurance policy that provided for the physical needs of my family. To some extent, that made life easier on Summer and those two. But money is never fair compensation for loss of life, loss for what could have been, loss of love.

Those two. Their story.

I'm uniquely qualified to tell their story. I lived with them, and I died surrounded by their love. In death, they are always before my eyes.

CHAPTER NINE

Toddrick waited by his locker. This wasn't the first time he'd had to wait. Jimmy was rarely on time for anything. Every morning, Toddrick had to push him out the door and help him get to class. There was a strong possibility that Jimmy would have missed out on his adolescent years if Toddrick hadn't dragged him through it all.

There were a few occasions when Jimmy was the first to appear. Meal times, mostly. Or when it was time to go to the movies or to the lake. He was selectively punctual, depending on the type of activity.

Another occasion when he could be counted on to be timely, or early, was when it was time to go home from school, like right now. Jimmy didn't mind getting to school late, but he was rarely late when it was over. The few times Jimmy didn't show up at the locker after school, Toddrick wandered the school halls and found him goofing off with some of his friends, or just milling around the boys locker room for who knows what.

Today, however, he was exceptionally late, and there

was no sign of Jimmy's friends creating a ruckus in the halls. Toddrick checked the boys locker room, but it was empty. He yelled in the girls locker room but got no response.

He looked at his watch and sighed. He shouldered his backpack and walked down the corridor to Jimmy's last period class, American history. Toddrick had been in Mr. Flannery's class on multiple occasions and had no troubles. But Jimmy had already had his share of problems with Mr. Flannery.

The door to Flannery's classroom was open. Toddrick poked his head in and saw Jimmy standing next to Mr. Flannery's desk. Flannery was leaning forward in his chair, cheeks as red as if he'd just run a marathon.

"You can't cheat on my tests," Flannery chided. He didn't just sound angry. Toddrick detected disappointment as well, a sad tone of pleading in the old man's voice. Almost like he was chastising and asking why at the same time. "You shouldn't cheat, period," he added in a softer tone. "Why?"

Jimmy's face was stone hard, his eyes fixed and defiant. Now I don't know much about how cheaters feel, but my guess is that most kids who've been caught cheating apologize or hang their head and show remorse. I would, especially if I'd been caught.

Not Jimmy. He looked straight back at Flannery, never breaking eye contact. "I don't see why I can't use books. You do! Every day you sit there and read your books, and then you give us the lessons." Jimmy took out a piece of paper from his pocket and held it up. "Well, I take notes. Why shouldn't I be allowed to use them?"

Flannery leaned back in his chair, his eyes narrowing. He looked like he was evaluating Jimmy's comment.

"Besides," Jimmy said, slightly less defiant, "it's not like I can't find anything out on the internet anyway. I can look up anything on my phone. In real life, it wouldn't be a problem. You have a question, you either know the answer or you look it up. Why is this different? Because I'm in your classroom? Because I have to abide by your rules?"

"You need to put information in your head." Flannery spoke through clenched teeth. He pointed a finger to his head, providing a visual demonstration as to where Jimmy needed to house information. "That is the point of testing you. I use these books as a point of reference." Flannery waved his hand over the books on his desk.

Jimmy cocked his head back like he'd been punched in the chin. "That makes no sense. Why do I have to remember everything and you don't?   If you can use the books as a point of reference, why can't I? Isn't what I'm doing a good way to learn too?"

Aside from the fact that he was being completely and utterly disrespectful, Jimmy had a point. I was pleased he could articulate a potential double standard. But at the same time, I would have liked my thirteen-year-old to show more respect for his teacher.

The shade of Flannery's face went from red to purple. I thought he was going to have a heart attack.

Toddrick stepped inside the room and cleared his throat. Mr. Flannery spotted him, and immediately his countenance changed. The stress he'd been containing in his face and neck released, and his natural pasty color returned.

Toddrick glanced at Jimmy, and their eyes met. Jimmy shook his head and rolled his eyes in a way that meant he was being wrongfully interrogated.

"Mr. Todd." Flannery noisily blew air out his nostrils. "We have ourselves a predicament." He waved his hands at Todd. "Come in, come in."

Toddrick walked toward the desk, his expression pensive. "Okay. I'm all ears."

"Of course you are."

Flannery smiled and held up a piece of paper. Toddrick leaned over the desk and looked at it. On one side, there was a list of numbers running down the page. After each number, there were a few sentences. At the top of the page there was a word written in bold: *Answers to Flannary's test.*

"I found this under Jimmy's desk during my test today. He was cheating."

Toddrick raised his eyes. That wasn't exactly what Jimmy had said. He'd stated that he was using his notes. It even sounded like a valid argument, but now that didn't look like the real issue. This was definitely an answer sheet with numbers on it.

The moral strength of Jimmy's point was gone.

Toddrick looked at Jimmy, who neither confirmed nor denied the charge, just stared back at him. Toddrick knew Jimmy even better than I did, and we both knew that if Jimmy was innocent, he would have said so. When Jimmy pleaded the fifth or remained silent, it could only mean one thing: guilty as charged.

Toddrick looked up from the answer sheet at Flannery. "What are you going to do? Mom won't be happy." At this last statement he looked at Jimmy, who, for the first time, looked uncomfortable.

Flannery sighed. "What am I supposed to do? I can't tolerate cheating." He looked down at his desk. "But I don't want to disappoint your mother. Lord knows you boys have been through a lot." His eyes pivoted back and forth between them. "Jimmy, I've given you chance after chance. I have enough history with you to get you expelled. And I have a mind to do just that!" He leaned back in his chair. "Tell me, what would your father do if he was still around?"

"Dad would give him a whooping," Toddrick answered. He got that right. I'd definitely give him a whooping. If not for the cheating, for the disrespect.

Flannery nodded. "Yes, well, *I* can't do that."

"I can." Toddrick eyed Jimmy.

Jimmy smiled skeptically. He shook his head at Toddrick. "No, you can't."

Toddrick rolled his eyes. "I'll whip you so fast you won't know what hit you."

"Not a chance," Jimmy said.

"Whoa, whoa," Flannery interrupted. His voice grew in excitement and a fire appeared in his eyes. The corners of his mouth drifted upward until they slowly formed a smile.

"Boys, I could get in big trouble for this." Flannery laughed. "But I think I'd like to see you get a whooping." He pointed at Jimmy. "I know I can't do it. I'm too old and you'd probably be the one to give me a whooping instead. There's also the fact that I'd get fired and lose my pension, which is almost mine. I'm retiring next year."

Flannery rested his hands across his belly. "Jimmy," Flannery looked directly at him in a fatherly way. "I don't want you to get in trouble, but you have to learn to swim on your own. You can't depend on those around you to pick you up. Toddrick won't always be there to save you when you're sinking."

There was silence before Flannery spoke again. "This is my price, Jimmy. But no one else needs to know. Just the three of us. Take your punishment from him," Flannery pointed to Toddrick, "or take it from me. Expulsion from school and everything that goes with that, or a whooping from your brother?

As an outsider looking in, I can see how one could question Flannery's methodology. Flannery was an old-fashioned man who grew up in a time when discipline was dished out with belts and paddles. He believed discipline in our modern society was slipping and kids were getting away with more and more every year.

"Are you serious?" Jimmy looked at Flannary in disbelief. Flannery's only response was raised eyes.

Jimmy looked at Toddrick, who was smiling. "One of us will get a whooping, but it ain't gonna be me," Jimmy threatened. "I'll take the whooping, but don't be disappointed if it doesn't go the way you want it."

Toddrick laughed.

"Where?" Flannery asked, too much excitement in his voice.

Jimmy pointed out the window. "Right there on the grass. You can watch from up here, sicko."

Toddrick tapped Jimmy on the shoulder. "Hey, show some respect. He's been more than good to you and you've been awful to him."

Mr. Flannery craned his neck toward the window and squinted at the area below, examining the view he would have. He put a hand to his mouth like he was thinking, maybe reconsidering what he was about to allow. He shook his finger at Jimmy. "Don't cheat anymore." His voice was forceful. "If it happens again, I'll get more people involved. Like the principle and your mother." He raised his eyebrows. "Are we clear?"

Jimmy didn't respond, so Toddrick did. "We're clear, sir."

Flannary's forehead crinkled. "What? No, no. I meant is the coast clear? I don't want anyone to see this." He looked out the window again and surveyed the scene. "It looks empty out there."

One minute later, Toddrick and Jimmy walked onto the grass beneath Flannery's window. They were behind the school, away from the traffic and secluded from view. School had been out for half an hour and no one was in sight. Toddrick and Jimmy both dropped their backpacks and looked at the window. Flannery stood there watching. He nodded at Toddrick in a "show him who's boss" kind of way.

As I've stated, those two were separated in age by less than a year, but Toddrick hit a growth spurt early on. Jimmy had grown little by little and was still waiting for his body to jolt upward—if it was going to at all.

They positioned themselves across from each other in a fighting stance. Even from my angle, the match looked uneven in Toddrick's favor.

They bounced around on their feet as they jockeyed for position. Then in a sudden and furious burst of energy, they collided. That Jimmy was smaller than Toddrick ended up not mattering. He fought with a ferocity that matched a mother bear defending her cub. Except Jimmy wasn't defending anything, he was just unleashing a hidden rage. He grabbed a hold of Toddrick's leg and drove forward, forcing Toddrick off the ground. Toddrick spent a few seconds suspended in the air before his body slammed down.

Toddrick rolled with the momentum and turned his

body right, repositioning himself away from Jimmy. He dove for Jimmy and snagged one of his feet. Jimmy strove to break free, but Toddrick smashed into his body, and they both fell. Toddrick took position on top of Jimmy, who began to squirm and wiggle like a worm, trying to free himself from strong hands.

Toddrick tried to trap Jimmy's flailing arms but was unsuccessful. The fury and swiftness of Jimmy's motion was as fast and strong as a practiced wrestler. In a few seconds, Jimmy was free and positioning his arms in front of his face like he was about to box. Toddrick positioned his hands the same way. With the exception of their difference in size, each was an exact mirror of the other.

Without taking his eyes off Jimmy, Toddrick reached into his back pocket and pulled out his phone. He tossed it on the ground near his bag. Jimmy did the same. It was an outward expression that the bout between them had escalated to the next level. This was serious now.

"You shouldn't cheat." Toddrick lunged forward with his arms and grabbed Jimmy's shoulders. Jimmy instinctively took the same position against his brother, and their arms locked. One pushed and the other pulled.

"It doesn't matter. I don't need to know half the junk they teach in that stupid building." Jimmy's face turned red with exertion. Toddrick was stronger, but Jimmy's will compensated for strength.

"Well, me neither, but you don't see me cheating," Toddrick said. His muscles strained beneath Jimmy's force. "You don't see anyone else cheating, do you?"

Jimmy's veins bulged, and Toddrick started to buckle

under the force. "Had enough?"

Toddrick shook his head. He dropped to his knees and turned Jimmy's weight against him. Jimmy's body flipped over Toddrick's back and slammed on the ground. Like lightning falling from the sky, Toddrick flung himself at Jimmy.

There was no time for Jimmy to react. Toddrick put Jimmy in a headlock and clamped his arms like vice grips around his neck. Toddrick breathed heavily in excursion as Jimmy struggled to escape.

I looked at my youngest, his cheeks pressed tight against Toddrick's arms, his face red from effort and little air. I'd felt sympathy for my boys often since I'd passed. They were going to struggle through life, which is hard no matter what, but they had to do it without a father. I know that millions of children do that, but it didn't stop me from feeling for them. Having someone and then not having them is different than never having someone at all. Those two knew loss.

In life, Jimmy had always been a mystery to me. There was something veiled about his feelings. And I could see that now more than ever before.

Jimmy was wrestling his brother, but his eyes told the story of a different fight. He was fighting a battle somewhere else, battling an unseen opponent. One you couldn't put your arms around, yet one that could hold you in the palm of its hand and squash you like a bug. From what I guessed, Jimmy was fighting himself; he was fighting the struggles of life.

Watching him all tied up in Toddrick's arms, I was suddenly sad. Saddened at the prospect of him being defeated. Not sad that he was going to lose to Toddrick, but sad at what this episode could represent. This struggle was indicative of life's battle, and life was going to be uncompassionate. Unlike Toddrick, Jimmy's real opponent didn't love him. Life knows not love.

Toddrick must have seen what I saw, the evidence of the war Jimmy was waging on existence. A well of tears broke like a tiny cloud, making a small rivulet of water run down Toddrick's face. A few of the liquid drops fell on Jimmy's skin, drawing his attention toward Toddrick.

Jimmy bucked his body and struggled against the pressure of Toddrick's grasp. As he did so, water broke from the mighty reservoir of Jimmy's frustration, and like his older brother, he too began crying.

"Say you won't cheat," Toddrick said as he tightened his grip around Jimmy's neck. His voice was strained and full of emotion. "Say it and I'll let go." His tears fell steadily.

Mr. Flannery knocked his hand against the window. "That's enough!" he shouted. "He's had enough. Toddrick, let go!"

"Say it!" Toddrick yelled louder, ignoring Flannery.

Jimmy's ability to breathe lessened as Toddrick clamped down. He reached up and tapped Toddrick's shoulder, the universal sign for "I'm done." Toddrick released his hold, and Jimmy gasped for breath, taking in giant gulps of air. They rolled off the ground, moving from their backs to their feet. Both bent over with hands on their knees and panting.

"Say you won't cheat." Toddrick's breathing was returning to normal, and the tears had stopped, though there was still wetness on his cheeks.

Jimmy looked at him and wiped moisture from his face. "Okay." He breathed heavily and dropped his head. "I won't cheat."

Toddrick nodded. He put his phone back in his pocket and shouldered his backpack. Jimmy was in the process of doing the same when Toddrick put his arms around him.

"Hey," he said. "I'm with you, bro." With one arm still hanging on Jimmy's shoulder, he spun and looked up to where Flannery had been watching. Flannery was standing in the open window, concern etched on his face.

"Did you hear that, Mr. Flannery? Did you hear what Jimmy said?"

Flannery nodded his head. "I heard.

 Jimmy!"

Jimmy turned and looked at the window.

"Chin up, lad. You're smarter and better than you let on." Flannery flashed a knowing smile and closed his window.

CHAPTER TEN

How is it that some kids act appropriately and others don't? How can some be so mean? I don't know what happens behind closed doors, but I assume all parents teach their kids to act a good way. The golden rule was the prevailing methodology when I was young. Treat others like you want to be treated. This attitude lends itself to kindness.

It's my assumption that mothers and fathers think the best of their kids, just like I do of mine. I also think that it's not uncommon for parents to believe it's their responsibility to *mold* their children. For lack of a better word, *train* them to exist in society. If our little ones behave in a way that is inappropriate or unseemly, we try and correct the behavior—set it right.

That's common. The norm.

What I can't seem to solve is why there are rotten kids who come from good parents, and good kids who come from rotten parents. How is it, if parents teach their children to be good and kind, that there end up being so many mean kids? There is no scientific model that says,

"Do this to your child and they will end up like this."

How is it that mothers and fathers do their best to ensure their children are brought up correctly, but we still get youth like Trent Maxwell? Again, I don't know what goes on behind closed doors, but I assume the Maxwell parenting method is similar to mine.

I know all children have learning curves and problems of their own. But Trent Maxwell was the definition of the word "problem." If Mr. Brentwood, the high school math teacher, was to pass out a test, every question could read, "Please solve this Trent Maxwell," and everyone would understand that they could substitute the word "problem" for "Trent."

There are Trents everywhere. But I guess it makes sense, because there are Toddricks everywhere too, right? Well, maybe not just like Toddrick. A few hopefuls, maybe. That's my fatherly pride coming through.

You see mean kids in movies all the time. Kids who lie and steal, kids who hurt others for Lord only knows why. On the screen, we see how they act, and we feel shocked and aggravated, outraged, even. They are usually the antagonist in the movie, the source of contention. I've often wondered if mean kids watching the movies associate themselves with those characters, or if they are blinded by their own warped perception. Do kids know they're jerks?

It's the rainbow spectrum of behaviors that affords us the opportunity to pick and choose who we like. How can there be a Trent without a Toddrick? Life would be a sad garden if only one type of vegetation existed. And so it is with human personality. Humans are the most diverse of all that inhabit the earth. A plush and multi-spectrum garden, filled with nice people, mean people, and all shades of in-between.

One would think that mean kids would be shunned from society, trapped in a cage of prolific detention, or at least separated from everyone else. Ironically, mean kids can function socially when they need to. They can blend in.

Trent, the meanest of them all, was an excellent chameleon. He knew when to be quiet, when to act interested or busy. He knew to be buttoned up around adults or parents. He could even keep it together when he was around girls he liked. But to everyone else, Trent was a nightmare.

His mouth was like a venomous cottonmouth snake. Except instead of poison, he spewed profanity in the most outrageous of streams. For whatever reason, his T-shirts usually displayed skulls or bones, and he wore black studded belts around his waist and hands. His clothes were so baggy, it was quite possible he was hiding a kitchen sink up his sleeves or down his trousers.

He was as mean as all get out. I mean really mean. If Jimmy was mean as a toddler, it was like being harassed by a dolphin in a pool, while Trent's mean was like being attacked by a shark off the coast of Alcatraz.

In the third grade, he kicked Lindsey Doyle in the back of the head and blamed it on an innocent bystander. Trent made such a compelling defense that both he and the innocent were punished for the violent act.

When he was in the sixth grade—again, I'll never understand why—he thought it would be funny to spend recess by the bike rack, emptying air from all the bike tires.

Trent wasn't deprived of virtues. He had the uncanny ability to make trouble and not get blamed for it. That's a rare talent, cultivated only by people who have a need to skate around the truth. The more lies you tell, the better you get at lying. He was a pro.

Now, I didn't spend my time watching Trent. He isn't my son. I didn't know any of this when I was alive, because I was minding my own family's business. But in death, you get new eyes that allow you to see other things: past, present, and some future.

I've got to be careful with what I say in regards to what life after death is like. There are rules about sharing things you're not supposed to around this place. You aren't kicked out or anything dramatic like that. But once you divulge something you're not supposed to, less knowledge is entrusted to you.

When it comes to seeing earthly things, I have the ability to rewind, as it were, and see things that involve my family. I get to see all things that affect my family. And believe you me. There are a million and one things that can go wrong but somehow don't. For that, I'm thankful.

Trent was one thing that went wrong in the lives of those two. He affected my family, so I've been given insight to his life. He was built like a brick house. Solid all the way around and as tough as nails. Why can't the mean guys be little skinny fellas? Why are they always some of the toughest kids alive?

One surly display of his atrocity happened in the boy's locker room at the high school. He snuck into a locker and applied a generous amount of muscle relaxer, the kind that burns like fire, into the jock strap of a young man. Unaware of the danger, the young man slipped into the athletic underwear and then into his tight football pants. By the time he realized his loins were on fire, it was too late.

Poor guy went into a panic, not knowing the cause of the volcanic heat on his reproductive organs. He hopped and crashed around as he removed his clothes, knocking over bystanders and slamming into lockers. He ended up in the fetal position on the floor, cradling his genitalia.

Trent laughed like a hyena through the entire ordeal. He didn't know it yet, but Trent was going to get his come-upin's on that one. There would be a big lawsuit in a few years. Philip Treasure, the young man whose groin was set ablaze, would suffer permanent side effects from the incident. Once Philip discovered the incident caused infertility, he would litigate against Trent and the school. It would get pretty ugly.

It's best to keep things that happen in the boys' locker room in the boys' locker room. If the world knew the depth of what goes on in those dark and unregulated areas, there would be an outcry for surveillance. Big Brother cameras would be put in place to make sure those dungeons got their images revamped. I think most people just accept the degradation associated within those areas of the school and choose to ignore it. Perhaps we hope our children don't hear the jokes and innuendo or don't witness the acts of betrayal or indecency.

It should be no surprise, then, that a high percentage of Trent's mischief took place in the locker room.

On another occasion in the locker room, Trent found himself alone with a little bitty freshman. Trent left the locker room, but little bitty freshman spent the whole of a two-hour football practice duct-taped to the bottom of a bench.

Again, I'll never understand it. Why he even had duct tape in his locker is a mystery.

As I think about Trent and those like him, my head and neck immediately tense up. I have to force myself to relax and remember that they're not normal. The greatest remedy for the anxiety I feel about Trent's type is the knowledge that there are people who are not like him. There are opposites of his callousness and cruelty.

Through elementary and middle school, Toddrick and Jimmy walked to and from school. It was a mile one-way, and the path was safe and well-known. For nearly eight years, they tread the same path. Consequently, they were very familiar with the terrain around their school and neighborhood.

High School was different. Extracurricular activities demanded that Toddrick and Jimmy drove themselves places. Besides, the high school was nearly three miles away from home.

Once or twice, the car wasn't available for their use. On those occasions, when their mother couldn't help them with transportation, they'd walk home.

Maybe they were meant to walk home that Tuesday afternoon. Maybe the car was meant to be in the shop that day.

"If we run, we can get home faster," Jimmy said. It had been a full year and a half since he entered high school, but he still hadn't grown much. So the bag full of books weighed him down. He thought moving faster along the grassy trail would ease the dull, consistent pressure on his legs. The faster they got home, the faster it would end.

Toddrick was content at the steady pace but didn't want Jimmy to feel like he was being ignored. "You can run ahead if you want. Or I can carry your bag for you if you can't make it." His voice was saturated with sarcasm. He was egging Jimmy on, something he liked to do when it was just the two of them.

"I can punch you in the mouth," Jimmy responded, shrugging his shoulders to shift the weight of the bag to a more comfortable spot. "How's that sound?"

Toddrick laughed. "Then you really would have to run. Say, have you ever thought about how close our house is to the school, as the crow flies?"

"What do you mean?" Jimmy crinkled his brow and breathed heavily. Sweat beaded down his forehead. "Why would I think about that? I'm not a crow."

"Think about it," Toddrick said. "It takes us twenty minutes to drive home, but we can run home in the same amount of time if we stick to the trails and back roads. We avoid all the traffic and obstacles by foot."

Jimmy looked at Toddrick skeptically. "I hate math. Is this a math problem? As the crow flies . . . what?"

"We have to drive all the way up that hill," Toddrick swept his arm in the direction of the hillside to their left, "and then come back down half of it just to get to our house. Or if you go the other way, you have to take the bridge all the way over the river." He looked over his shoulder and pointed to the school through the trees. "Look, the school is just right there," he turned back in the direction they were walking, "and home is just right there. It can't be more than a couple miles. How fast can you run a couple miles?"

"I don't see why it matters to . . ." Jimmy's voice

trailed off. He was looking into the trees that dotted the hillside, his attention drawn there by Toddrick's gesture. "Who is that?" He pointed toward the trees.

Behind the timbers and the shadows they cast, hardly visible, were four profiles. It was hard to see what they were doing beyond the concealment of the trees.

The humanoid shapes were meshing in and out of each other, making it impossible to tell who was doing what, or whether it was playful or destructive activity.

Toddrick began to jog toward the trees. "Now you want to run?" Jimmy shouted. "Where are you going?"

"I'm just going to check it out," Toddrick yelled over his shoulder. "It looks exciting."

Jimmy grunted and shifted the weight of his bag onto the opposite shoulder. "I could probably run a few miles in a few minutes," he mumbled under his breath, "if I didn't have this stupid bag." He ran several steps in Toddrick's direction. "Or a brother who didn't chase squirrels."

The closer they got to the trees, the clearer the shapes became. Inside the shadows, Trent and two other nameless lackeys (sometimes evil travels in packs) were pushing Brett Waskom. Between the three boys, Brett looked like a bouncing ball in a pinball machine. He made a few attempts to go between two of his tormentors, but they latched onto his arms, one on each side. He struggled to free himself but got tossed back in the center of the terrible triangle.

Toddrick turned around and faced Jimmy. "If this goes bad, drop your bag and run home."

Jimmy rolled his eyes and shook his head. "Right," he said sarcastically.

"I mean it." Toddrick didn't wait for Jimmy to reply.

He entered the grove of trees, and Trent spotted him.

"Hey, guys. What's going on?" Toddrick asked. He addressed everyone, but he was staring at Trent.

The pin-balling stopped, but nobody responded. "Nothing, Todd," Trent said, acting as voice for the suddenly timid group. "Just having a little fun."

Toddrick's expression was flat, like he wasn't buying that anything taking place here was fun. He looked at the pinball. "You having fun, Brett?"

"No," he said, his voice a little shaky. "Trent wants to fight me. I ain't done nothing and I don't wanna fight nobody. I just wanna go home." Brett was a sophomore, the same grade as Jimmy. But unlike Jimmy, he'd hit his growth spurt two years earlier. Shot up like a tree. Only he was soft and uncoordinated. Maybe he looked like he could defend himself, but a closer look showed his muscles were untrained and lackluster.

"Okay, Brett," Toddrick responded, pointing to the nearest cluster of houses, "go home."

Brett took a few tentative steps outside the triangle of fury. His eyes were uncertain, almost like he expected to become the pinball again.

"Hold on," Trent said. "He just can't leave. Not without a replacement. You volunteering?" Trent poked his chin at Todd.

Toddrick dropped his bag. "You bet." There was no more talking, no hesitation and no philandering. By the look on Trent's face, he hadn't expected such a response.

Toddrick launched into Trent's chin with his right hand, and a resounding crack filled the air. Trent fell backward and landed on his rump. Toddrick shook his hand, obviously hurt from the bone on bone contact. He rubbed his knuckles and winced.

The two lackeys who'd helped torment Brett took a few steps back, unclear about what they were supposed to do. It was clear they were truly mindless followers. Now that they were not the aggressors, they looked particularly weak.

Trent got up from the ground. He cursed as he spit a mixture of blood and saliva from his mouth. He charged Toddrick while flailing his arms in an unorganized pattern. His wide swings missed Toddrick. It was awkward to watch.

Trent talked tough and big, picked on kids younger than him and loved doing things to people behind their backs. But by the looks of it, it was very possible that he'd never actually had to defend himself. His dastardly deeds had been against those weaker than himself or done in secret. Toddrick, on the other hand, had plenty of practice, mostly in defense of Jimmy or from Jimmy himself. Toddrick's hands were in front of his face like a professional boxer, his elbows tucked in close to his body and his legs poised like springs.

After dodging Trent's wild swings, Toddrick stepped forward. With each step he took, he landed a solid jab somewhere on Trent's face. They weren't crushing blows, just stunning jabs. I don't know if Toddrick really knew how to hurt somebody, or if he just didn't want to. The punches he landed on Trent did little damage beyond a bloody nose or a split lip.

Blood, frustration, and anger were visible on Trent's face. He screamed like a maniac and dashed at Toddrick, who sidestepped the charging bull and extended his leg. Trent tripped over Toddrick's shoe and fell face-first into the grass.

He groaned and lifted his body off the ground. Toddrick stepped on top of his shoulder, holding him down. "Don't get up. Not yet." Under the weight of Toddricks foot, Trent's body fell back down. "Just leave people alone. We're leaving now, and I don't want you to follow us. You three can have your fun with each other." Toddrick retrieved his bag. "Come on, Jimmy."

Jimmy puffed out his chest and stepped next to one of Trent's cronies. "Yeah. We'll go home now, son." Jimmy stood up on his toes to get as close to the kids nose as possible.

The boy smacked Jimmy on the back of the head, like a dad might smack his kid for disobeying. Not really an act meant to hurt Jimmy, just to insult him. As Toddrick walked by, he pushed the boy, letting him know that Jimmy was off-limits.

"He started it," the boy defended.

"Jimmy," Toddrick scolded, "please, leave the bullies alone."

CHAPTER ELEVEN

Dances in the days of my youth were preceded by excitement and anticipation. In those days, decades ago, you didn't need to coax kids to dress up in their Sunday best and go to a dance. There was plenty of gossip about who was going with who and who'd asked who and who'd been rejected. We wanted to dance, and kids wanted to be seen dancing. There were wall-flowers for sure, but they attended the dances in hope that they would be an active participant in the festivities.

Now a day, from what I can see, dances aren't really dances at all. Hardly anyone knows how to dance; they only sway from side to side, and they're not even good at that. I wouldn't want to go to a dance either if all you did was listen to music in a dark room and sway. Boring.

But I suppose the reason we don't see a lot of good dances is because that is a symptom of a larger problem. My children live in an outrageously bold time. It's wonderful, but nothing is sacred or private. I think kids know that, so they shun anything that can expose how they feel.

In this age of infinite music, sexual progressiveness, and video games, it seems like kids don't want to form lasting relationships. Dancing is intimate. You have to look someone in the eye for at least three minutes, and if you're bold enough, you can talk.

Eye contact and conversation. No text messages. No electronic devices. Rough.

Today, the connection that can only be achieved through human interaction has been replaced by cheap and impersonal online meetings and blinking lights on a screen. For many, technology has replaced communication and friendship.

Those social events that once bound us together, the ones that forced awkwardness out of everyone and strengthened the human connection, are slowly being replaced by any kind of social media out there. I'm not saying those applications are bad. But they aren't meant to replace human interaction, rather to enhance it. Somehow I don't think that's happening.

Dancing used to mean something—a boy and a girl holding hands and stepping to the music. Or a girl and a boy trying to swing their arms and kick their legs in unison while a musical beat propelled them onward. It was a fun and flirtatious atmosphere.

Technology isn't the only reason modern adolescents don't get the dancing scene. A contributing factor that is fundamentally different is the music. Mainstream music in my time was consistent among the youth. There were a few popular artists and groups that filled the air ways. There was also limited access to music. It was either on the radio or television. We all heard the same stuff.

Not today. There are so many types of music to choose

from. Not that this is a bad thing, but you can listen to rock, rap, classic rock, metal, trash metal, indie, pop, hip hop, blue grass, country, gangsta and scores more genres of music. Getting a few hundred kids together and trying to find a common denominator in musical taste is near impossible.

A lot of the music I hear isn't conducive to holding hands and dancing on a gym floor. What I do hear is closer to the sound track of what transpires on a wedding night between husband and wife. Or worse, what happens in the lowest of moral dens like strip clubs, whore houses, and shady massage parlors. All that is pounded out to rhythmic drums. Pretty sexual. And have you tried dancing to it? Music has become a catalyst for pervasiveness, a gateway drug to sex. Not all, but much of today's music is dipped in sensuality.

Keeping an eye on those two boys afforded me the opportunity to see dancing through their eyes and their culture norms. Frankly, it scared me. Slow dances cleared the floor, and nobody wanted to be seen dancing with a partner. Unless, of course, you were going steady with someone. And then, your dancing was bear hugging in the middle of the floor. Not really dancing, just groping.

Today, those that don't stay on the floor, those that don't have someone to hug during those slow songs, retreat to the side lines and flip through their phones. Forget about asking someone to dance. That takes courage, feeling and liveliness.

Fast songs pound away with crude and sexual lyrics that destroy any chance of an innocent mingling. Innuendo and encouragement of under-aged activities are all streaming into young ears. And from there to their minds. It's only a matter of time before you do what you think. Thoughts give birth to action.

What streams out of those speakers today would have made my generation, and without a doubt the generations before, blush and run for home and chapel.

Sexuality is nothing new, but we tried to respect it a little more. Not hide it or pretend it didn't exist. Just keep it in the proper place and time. At least, the majority of people did. In today's world, the pendulum has swung the opposite direction, and those that openly flaunt sexuality vastly outnumber those that keep it sacred.

Toddrick and Jimmy's generation didn't shy away from the outward appearance of sex and publicly accepted what my generation considered immoral. I'm amazed parents and society allowed it.

Somewhere there is a plan for course correction.

Would you look at me? Rattling on like my opinion is important.

Those two. Their story.

At one such inappropriate, gyrating and hip-swishing prom dance, Toddrick and Jimmy partook in the festivities. Toddrick, of course, took the sweetheart of his youth, Lisa Betford. She'd grown up pretty and bright. She laughed at how silly everyone was at these dances but could enjoy herself amidst the weirdness of it all. She had a sober mind and a good heart, just like Toddrick. They fit together.

It took Jimmy longer than normal, but he grew into his body and became a handsome cuss. He was all fun and no commitment. Consequently, he had a healthy cluster of female friends. Quite by accident, he'd developed a reputation for providing a good time, and in a good way. He had his pick of any girl, and tonight's selection was Stacey McMullen. More than one boy turned green when they discovered he'd be going to prom with Stacey. A junior taking a senior to prom was hard to pull off.

In the midst of all the jumping and dancing around on this prom night, Jeannette Applewood guided her wheelchair onto the dance floor. She was alone.

Jeanette Applewood. Daughter of Jed and Julie Applewood. I've known the Applewoods ever since Summer and I moved to Greenly, Arkansas. Jed helped unload the moving truck when I pulled up to our newly purchased house. He saw that Summer was pregnant and that I was by myself. He didn't hesitate to sacrifice his Saturday helping his new neighbors move in. The Applewoods; lifelong friends and current neighbors to my family.

Jed was tall and thin, but strong-limbed. When we met him and his wife, they were expecting an addition to their family, just like Summer and me. It was fun to see both Summer and Julie walking around with large bellies, trading stories and troubles. Both women were tiny, small enough that their growing bellies made them look down-right inhuman. Julie and Summer spent many a day together during those mutually maternal months. And Jed was nice enough company for me.

Toddrick and Jeannette were born within a month of each other.

Julie Applewood's pregnancy had a few complications, and baby Jeanette was born with severe cerebral palsy. Jed and Julie, having tried for years to have children without success, were pleased to have Jeannette in their lives. Julie quit her job and took care of Jeanette full-time—poured her life into that little girl.

Jeannette, or Jean, as she was called by those who knew her, attended the same school as those two boys. The school had a special-needs division with curriculum for functional development. She wasn't the only one in the school who spent her days in a wheel chair, but Jean was definitely the most advanced in her condition.

By the time high school rolled around, Jean had developed the ability to speak. It was hard to understand her because she couldn't enunciate well. Her mind was as sharp as any, but it was a challenge to make her mouth say what she wanted. Each word was a monumental task, and you could see the concentration on her face as she forced her mouth to move. Truthfully, she sounded like she was drunk all the time.

Conversation with Jean was exhausting. Not for you, for her. Every sound took energy out of her, every finished word drained her. By the end of one sentence, she looked like she was ready to collapse from exhaustion. It took patience and practice to communicate with her.

Through the diligence of her mother, Jean gained motor skills and hand-eye coordination beyond the norm for her condition. Consequentially, she was able to move about the school by way of a battery powered wheelchair. The chair must have weighed a thousand pounds and could travel at a speed of ten miles an hour. Something that heavy and moving that fast down the hallway could be quite impressive or scary, depending on whether or not you were in Jean's way. One of her hands gripped a small toggle switch, with which she could navigate turns and move forward or backward.

Life had given Jean hard things, but she'd learned to

do all right on her own.

Toddrick's senior prom dance was also Jean's. People might think someone like Jean would shy away from public or social functions. Events like dances, or any occasion that requires legs and feet would be at the top of the list of things to avoid if you're in a wheelchair.

But normal people weren't Jean.

Jean toggled her chair onto the glossy gymnasium floor. With no date or dance partner, she directed her chair into the closest group of romping teens. Kids didn't flee before her as I expected.

The music was fast and strong, and the teens bobbed up and down to the rhythm. Jean would have jumped and bobbed if she could have, but obviously she couldn't. Instead, she moved the toggle switch on her chair to the left and right, over and over. Quite by accident, the swing of the chair caused Jean's legs to bump into the boy standing to her right, and then the girl standing to her left.

The boy handled it fine, but the girl's expression betrayed annoyance from the untimely and repetitive thumping of Jean's legs. By the looks of it, she didn't want to be rude, so the girl slowly took a few steps backward and joined a neighboring group of teens. Over the course of that one song, the group around Jean dwindled, each person methodically meshing into a neighboring group, until Jean was alone again.

No one tried to be mean. It just happened.

The music transitioned from the fast-paced rhythm to a slow and romantic melody. You'd have thought the dance was suddenly over as the floor emptied. There were a few people here and there, the steady couples.

Jean had already been left alone, but her aloneness

had been camouflaged by the multitude of the jumping bodies that surrounded her. With the floor clear, it was easier to see that she was by herself.

"Lisa?" Toddrick had a few creases between his eyes. It was his trademark look of concern.

She moved her head off his chest and looked up. "What?" She was smiling until she caught a glimpse of his expression. "What's wrong?"

He shrugged his shoulders. "Nothing, really." He pointed his chin toward Jean. She was sitting in her chair near the center of the gym. "Do you see Jean?"

Lisa turned her head and looked. "Yes."

"I want to ask her to dance." He cleared his throat. "You'll be without a partner for a bit."

Lisa examined Toddrick through slit eyelids. "You're gonna ask her to dance?" She sounded skeptical.

"If it's okay with you. How many times will she get to dance tonight? How many times does she get to dance with a boy who isn't her dad?" He looked expectantly at Lisa.

Lisa stopped swaying and looked at Toddrick, who raised his eyes expectantly. Her lips parted, and it looked like she was about to interrogate him. She closed her mouth and nodded her head. "Of course you can ask her."

Toddrick eyed her, trying to interpret her tone. Maybe she was teasing him. "You seem a little uncertain," he said.

"No." Lisa shook her head. "I think it's really sweet. She deserves more than one dance." She smiled. "What will you do if she turns you down?" She cocked an eyebrow.

Toddrick smiled and ignored her joke. "Great. I might

be able to get her to do more than one dance."

"You're not going to dance with her all night, are you?" she asked as he walked away.

He looked back at her and winked. "Nope."

Toddrick approached Jean, who had stopped toggling back and forth in her chair. It had been a while since he'd talked to her. He knelt down next to her chair.

"Jean," he yelled over the music. "Would you like to dance?"

Her head fell forward and then reared back as if she was nodding. The movement was so pronounced that it looked like it might hurt her neck. Her lips moved slowly upward until they formed a smile. Jean's brow furrowed and her lips tightened. Her words came out slow but very succinct. "Yes! Undo my belt." Around her waist, Jean wore a seat belt that kept her safely fastened to her chair. "Pick me up."

Having been neighbors all their lives, Toddrick had seen Jean lifted out of her chair a hundred times by her father, so he knew it could be done. Someone who didn't know her so well would have been more tentative to take her out of her chair, but Toddrick reached down and pressed the release on the belt buckle.

Now, I'd lifted Jean out of her chair a few times when I was helping Jed around the house. It surprised me at how heavy she was. Jean couldn't latch on or try and distribute her weight like most children could. No draping her arm around your shoulder or putting her legs around your back. She was dead weight, and dead weight is heavy. I doubted Toddrick was prepared for how heavy Jean would be.

As he hefted her from the chair, I looked for a sign of strain in his face and neck, but I saw none. He situated her in his arms like a groom would carry a bride over the threshold of a door and started to sway back and forth to the music.

"Jean?" Toddrick asked. Her head rested in the crook of his elbow and she leaned against his arm.

She concentrated as she replied, making her face tighten and constrict. "Yes." Her head lifted off his arm and fell back down.

"I'm not a great conversationalist, and I'm using most of my strength to hold you up." He adjusted her in his arms, shifting weight from one arm so the other could take a break. "I hope you don't mind if I don't talk much."

Jean smiled. "No problem." Her eyes crossed as she concentrated. "Don't drop me."

Now, Toddrick didn't do things to be seen. It wasn't his way. But something tells me he knew a few people would be watching, and when he said that he was hoping Jean would get more than one dance, I think he had a plan in mind.

Across the gym, Jimmy was standing with his date. Like everyone else, he'd been taking regular breaks during the slow songs, trying to avoid the intimate human connection. As he got a drink, he saw Toddrick lift Jean out of her chair. He watched them sway together through the entire song. When the music transitioned to a faster beat, he watched Toddrick place Jean back in her chair and buckle her belt around her waist. Before Toddrick walked away from her, he bent down and kissed her on the cheek.

People see things. Sometimes, they imitate what they see others do. Good or bad.

The next slow song, Jimmy knelt beside Jean's

wheelchair and asked her to dance. Like Toddrick, he lifted her out of the chair and began to sway with the music.

After his dance with Jean, Jimmy made a quick challenge to a half dozen of his friends. He declared they weren't strong enough to dance with Jean for an entire slow song. "My arms were throbbing halfway through the song," he claimed. "None of you weaklings could do it."

Well, Jean's night was one she would never forget. It was also one I'll never forget. A few seconds into every slow song, there was a young man at Jean's side, unlatching her belt and hoisting her into the air. She was not without a dance partner for the entire night.

CHAPTER TWELVE

E veryone handles liquor a little differently. I know some who've sworn the stuff off completely, and there are others who enjoy the casual glass of wine now and again. I know others who enjoy their alcohol like I enjoyed good food . . . a lot. And then there were a few sad ones who couldn't get enough of it. Eternally thirsty. At some point in their lives, it smashed them like a hammer smashes a nail. The strength of their addiction drove them straight through a job, through their families, and through life.

Alcohol consumption was not a part of my family's life. Summer and I didn't drink, so it was never in our house.

I've seen good people ruin their lives without any help from alcohol. I've also seen alcoholics accomplish greater things in life than I would aspire to. Alcohol isn't evil and neither are those who drink it.

However, I've seen a lot of good people do stupid stuff under the umbrella of an intoxicant. I've been around a lot of people while they've been drunk or in various stages of drunkenness. Sometimes it's been fun and sometimes it's been downright dangerous.

For me and mine, it was best to avoid it. That's what my Dad taught me, and that's how I taught those two.

I've already mentioned how small people pretend to be big people. And there aren't very many better examples than in the department of alcohol consumption. By law, it's an adult thing. Adults are supposed to be mature enough to regulate their own booze.

Sometimes it doesn't matter how mature you are. Booze is booze.

I once followed a story on CNN about a newscaster who struggled with a choice: introduce alcohol to their child at home, or let them experience it unsupervised with their friends.

I remember shaking my head and laughing at the situation. The discussion was never about breaking or honoring the law, or teaching your child to wait for the legal age. The news article never debated moral correctness; it sought to answer the question of who should introduce the child to alcohol, the parent or society. Like it was a given that the child was going to drink alcohol regardless of whether or not they were of legal age.

Well, Toddrick and Jimmy weren't introduced to it at my home, but sure enough, they had plenty of exposure elsewhere.

It was the summer of Toddrick's senior year. Early morning football practice had them up at sunrise, driving to the football fields. The sun was not completely awake yet, but what light was available reflected off the morning dew.

Jimmy, who was half-sleeping in the passenger side,

spotted a girlish figure stumbling along the side of the road. It immediately woke him up. "Look at that." He pointed out the window and tapped the glass with his finger. "Do you see her?"

Toddrick slowed the vehicle and looked to the side of the road. "Whoa. It's too cold to be walking around dressed like that."

She walked a few feet off the side of the road, hidden by the shadow of a nearby steep embankment. Her movement was choppy and uncoordinated. The way she walked made her look like a tiny lady Frankenstein, lifting legs without bending at the knees and moving her arms up and down as if she were a marionette. She looked unnatural, uncomfortable and cold.

The only clothes she wore were a pair of boxer shorts that barely covered her backside, a loose-fitting white tank top, and a sock. No shoes, no sandals, just one dirty white tube sock. Hardly enough clothes for a chilly morning. Her matted hair had a dull lumpiness to it, like it had been rubbed with dirt or something sticky.

"I think her legs hurt or something," Jimmy said. "She's walking funny." He cocked an eyebrow. "But she's still kind of hot."

"She's almost naked!" Toddrick exclaimed. "She has to be freezing. Where are her shoes?"

"Yeah. No clothes," Jimmy repeated. "You think she's hot, too?"

Toddrick punched Jimmy's arm. "That's not what I was thinking." Toddrick sighed and nodded his head. "Okay, she *is* cute. But she doesn't look good. What's the matter with her? Roll down your window and ask if she's okay."

Toddrick pulled the car to a stop, and Jimmy rolled

the window down. He leaned out the car. "Hey, miss. You okay?" His tone had the right amount of concern in it. One of the worst things those two could have done was make the girl feel like they were creeps looking to take advantage of stranded girl.

She struggled to maintain her balance. She turned toward Jimmy and examined him, her eyes searching for someone she recognized. Her mouth opened, but no words came out. She put her hands up, like she wanted them to wait for her, almost like she was afraid they were going to leave her. And then she hurled dull pink liquid from her mouth. It was a quick, one time wretch, but her already questionable balance was thrown off, and she fell on the ground.

Both doors of the car swung open as those two rushed to her side. Her body shook; either from the cold or something else, it was hard to tell. Toddrick and Jimmy scooped her up, one boy under each arm.

"How can we help?" Toddrick asked. "Do you need to see a doctor?"

"Her skin is freezing," Jimmy said as his hand lifted her shoulder. "You can't get hypothermia in Arkansas, can you?"

"We should take her to the hospital," Toddrick said. "Maybe we should call the police, too. They'll help, right?"

The girl shook her head. "No." Her voice was muddled and slurred. She licked her lips and smacked them together like she was chewing imaginary food. "No police." She rested her head on Jimmy's shoulder. "Coffee. Do you have any coffee."

The skin on Jimmy's forehead crinkled. "You want coffee?"

She nodded.

"Get her to the car," Toddrick said. "She needs to get warm. She can lie down in the back seat."

They placed her in the back of the car and turned the heaters on full blast. She sat crookedly, leaning heavily to one side. It looked like she was going to topple over at any second.

"Well," Toddrick said as he pushed on the gas pedal, "we're going to be late to practice. Where's the nearest Starbucks?"

"What's your name?" Jimmy looked in the back seat.

Her voice was quiet and breathy, her consonants sloppy and wet. "Melissa," she said, but it sounded like "Mflda."

"Melissa?"

She nodded her head.

"What happened to you?" Jimmy asked.

Melissa didn't respond. Her eyes were glazed over and she leaned against the door.

"It's all right," Jimmy soothed. "You can rest. We'll get you that coffee."

With hot coffee in her blood and the heat of the car beating down on her, Melissa became a little more sensible. "Thank you, guys." She sipped from her paper cup. "Do you mind taking me home?"

"No problem," Toddrick said. He pulled out of Starbucks and headed back in the direction where they picked her up. "We'll have you back in no time."

Melissa looked mortified. "Oh, don't take me back there. That's not my home. I never should have gone there."

"Um, okay. Where to?" Toddrick asked. "I'll follow your directions."

"To Riordan Hall, just off campus." She pointed toward the University. "Do you know where it is?"

Toddrick didn't. He followed her directions to a tall, brown-brick apartment complex. When the car stopped, Jimmy turned to her and smiled. "Here we are. Can I help you to your place?"

She shook her head and started to cry. Her shoulders trembled as she made tiny sobbing sounds. Both Toddrick and Jimmy tried to comfort her, but her crying persisted. The two boys looked back and forth at each other uncomfortably, not sure how to help or what was the matter.

When the crying subsided, Jimmy asked, "What's wrong? Did you forget where you live?"

Melissa cried again before she spoke, letting out a fresh torrent of tears. "I got stupid drunk last night. I don't have my purse, my shoes, or my clothes, and I feel sick. I want to throw up."

"It's okay," Jimmy said. "I ain't ever been drunk, but I think you can sleep these things off." He looked at Toddrick. "Right?" Toddrick shrugged his shoulders, and Jimmy turned back to Melissa. "Just go inside and take a nap." He pointed to the apartment complex. "These are college dorm rooms. That means you go to the University, right? You can do whatever you want."

She wiped away what remained of her tears. "You two are so nice. Nice boys don't let this happen to girls." She shook her head and sobbed again, her face twisting inward like she was sucking on a lemon. "I wasn't with nice boys last night." She opened the rear passenger door. "I'm so sorry. I'm so embarrassed."

"Don't worry about it," Jimmy replied, putting on a charming smile. "My name is Jimmy."

She gave a trembling, embarrassed smile, tears welling in her eyes again. "That's not what I mean. I'm sorry because I peed in your car."

A particularly strange introduction to drunkenness for those two. They would get many more opportunities to witness people under the influence of alcohol. For better and worse.

Toddrick and Jimmy, being respectively good-looking and nice boys, had a certain amount of popularity among their peers. They never were the *in-crowd* or the most pretentious, but they never lacked friends.

Toddrick wasn't flamboyant about his dislike of intoxicants, but he quietly ducked out of parties and situations when he noticed the bottles or cans come out. At such times, he would tell Jimmy he was going, but he never forced him to leave.

Jimmy followed Toddrick.

Every year, just before graduation, a large groups of kids went to a spot in the woods to celebrate the end of their lower level education. They lit a bonfire and got drunk. A splendid yearly tradition. Toddrick's friends wanted him there. And if Toddrick was invited, it was implied that Jimmy was too.

Toddrick took his usual stance on drinking parties. "You know I don't want to go," he said. "Last thing I want is to see my friends getting drunk out of their minds and acting like backwoods hillbillies. Besides, what if the cops come? Won't I be breaking the law by association or something?"

"Hey!" Jake Wacum shouted. "What's wrong with acting like hillbillies?" Jake playfully punched Toddrick on the arm. "Come on, man. Just this once."

Jake was one of Toddrick's closest friends. All their

years in grade school they'd sat next to each other. They goofed off together and were considered the unofficial class clowns. Outside of Jimmy, Jake was probably the closest person to Toddrick.

"Half the police officers are former high-schoolers here," Jake continued, "and they did the same thing. If they busted us for drinking, it would be the biggest hypocritical act of all time."

Toddrick smiled. "Love you guys, but I'm not going." They'd just finished track practice, and the team was changing their clothes in the locker room.

"You don't have to drink nothing." Brad Cederburg pulled on his shirt.

"Come on," someone asserted. "Just go to the party."

Suddenly, all the talk in the locker room went silent, and everyone focused on Toddrick. What started as a friendly conversation between Jake and Toddrick became a barrage of encouragement for Toddrick to attend the school's senior drunk fest. Even Jimmy sat and listened, not sure how it was going to end. There were a half dozen pleas and various types of come-ons, but Toddrick laughed them all away.

"Okay. I got it," Mark Domitrovich said, like he'd just thought of the best solution. He slapped his hand on the nearest locker. "Toddrick, you still go to that church, right? The one off Fifth Avenue?"

Toddrick nodded his head. He shot a glance at Jimmy and Jake, maybe wary that Mark was going to cross the line. "Yeah. So?"

"I haven't gone to church since I was ten years old," Mark said. "If you come with us to senior keg, I'll go with you to church." Mark closed his locker. "Once." He rolled his eyes at Toddrick. "I'll come with you once. That's a fair trade."

Toddrick looked like he was considering it.

"And," Mark's voice grew louder. Everyone was listening, and Mark loved to be the center of attention. "I'll make sure you get your own container of orange juice. You don't have to drink nothing else." Mark smiled proudly. "How is that for a deal? I go to church, and you go to senior keg."

Toddrick smiled. "Go to church one time? Hmm."

Mark nodded. "We all will." He tapped his two companions on the shoulder. Both Jake and Brad hesitated, shared an uncomfortable glance, and then nodded their heads in agreement. By the looks on their faces, it was clear they didn't like the verbal contract. They would either have to make themselves liars or church-goes. Apparently, neither one was appealing.

"Tell you what," Toddrick said. "You come to church every week until senior keg, and I'll go." There was three Sundays between then and senior keg. Toddrick reached in his locker and grabbed his keys. "But don't expect me to drink."

"No problem," Jake said.

"All three of you got to go." Toddrick looked at them. "But don't make a ruckus. I'm not a church nut, but I don't want you disturbing anybody who is." He started to walk up the stairs, and then turned and said, "Why do I get the feeling you think drinking and going to church are polar opposites? It's like you think drinkers are bad people and the chapel is for good people. But I don't think you're bad for drinking and I don't think church is only for those who don't."

"Wait," Jake said. "You don't think we're bad for drinking?"

"Stupid." Toddrick winked. "And a criminal, but not a bad person."

Jimmy, who was pulling up the rear of the group, chimed in. "Think of it like this. We're at school, but we don't care about learning. We're here because we have to be. How is church any different? People go all the time, sit and listen, say things, sing songs and do whatever, but they don't really care. They're there because they have to be."

The group stopped walking and looked at Jimmy. He wasn't known for making sense or good comparisons, so when he said stuff that made a little bit of sense he got people to listen. "I hate going to school, sitting and pretending like I'm listening about blah blah blah who knows what. And who cares? You going to church so that someone will go to a party isn't any worse than going to school and not learning. The building is just a shell, anyways." Jimmy started walking up the stairs. "Hardly anyone in church is really good, just like hardly anyone in this school is really educated."

Now, down in these parts of the United States, we consider ourselves part of the Bible Belt. Lots of Christians and lots of Bible thumpers. And all different shades of Christians, too. 'Round here, you can be saved by a Christian and mugged by a Christian in the same day. Some people take it real serious, and others not.

Jimmy went to church every Sunday and held his head in his hands the entire time. I'm pretty sure he was sleeping most of the time. Yet, something told me his ears were tuned into everything that was said. Maybe even more so than those that shout "Amen" or sing their lungs out.

There was a group of kids at the high school who were

a proudly professing group of stalwart Christians. Every morning they gathered round the flag pole to pray. They also met for Bible study at lunch or after school. They considered themselves to be mini-preachers, evangelicals among the sinners.

An agreement was made. Toddrick would go to senior keg if his three friends Jake, Brad, and Mark attended church the next three Sundays.

The first Sunday rolled around and no Jake, Brad, or Mark. Not surprising. Maybe Toddrick was making a calculated wager when he made the deal. Perhaps he knew they wouldn't come, so he wouldn't have to go to senior keg.

Those three no showing wasn't a big surprise, but something did happened that surprised me.

The conversation in the locker room had been heard by all. Whether they wanted to see if Jake would live up to his end of the deal, or if they were just looking for an open invitation, four young men had enough curiosity to meet Toddrick at church that Sunday.

And wouldn't you know it. To this day, two of the four still go. Regularly and actively.

Those two weren't holy rollers or die-hard missionaries. But at least they weren't deterrents.

CHAPTER THIRTEEN

Considering we only get a hundred years to live, roughly, each year of our life is crucial. Think of years as if they were dollars. One hundred dollars isn't very many. It can be spent in a minute, lost faster than it came and with nothing to show for it. They come and go. Fast.

You can get more money when you run out. Being broke is temporary. Running out of years to live is a different situation. It's not so easy to come by years once they are gone.

It's difficult to say which years are the most important. All the years of our lives, every single one, is invaluable. Every learning stage, every working stage... all of them.

To the living, I'd say the most important year of your life is the one you're living right now.

The years when a young man leaves his home are among the most crucial. He steps out from under the care of a guardian and becomes his own protector. He covers his own nakedness, puts a roof over his own head, takes an accounting of his own money, gets his own cell phone plan, and sets his own schedule. Sink or swim, live or die.

Some young adults handle the freedom like five-year-old kids. They run off and go crazy with indulgence in whatever it was they couldn't get at home and shirk all responsibility. Their parents, their past providers, their life-long caregivers, somehow wronged them and were unjust rulers. They act like moms and dads established arbitrary rules with tyranny and suppression.

Freedom comes when boys and girls venture out on their own and make decisions and work for themselves. That is the greatest time in a person's life. It is also the greatest test.

Running away from Mom and Dad so you can party isn't freedom. Just a poor imitation of it. Spending your summer months behind a television and playing video games isn't real life, either. Mom and Dad know that, and that's precisely why they didn't allow it. Or shouldn't allow it.

Freedom is the ability to work and turn your work into exchangeable goods. Freedom is the ability to create your situation through your own choices. To be rich or poor by your own efforts, to develop your conscience according to your own desires and actions. That's freedom. That's the South. That's America.

I always admired the kids who had jobs during high school. They had an early start on real life experience and money management. If I'd been around, I probably would have made Toddrick and Jimmy work a little more.

After graduation, Toddrick had a brief respite before he took off to begin his collegiate studies. He was anxious to learn about other cultures and see the United States outside of a Southern lens. He'd been accepted into a program designed to expose students to the social norms and issues of different regions around the world. It was an intense study abroad program.

The university gave program options: six months, one year, or two years. With whatever package chosen, the student would have to take a full semester worth of classes in addition to the study program and proposed culture assimilation. Whether to participate in the program wasn't a difficult decision for Toddrick. Getting out and seeing more of the world was something he'd always wanted to do. What was difficult was deciding how long he would be abroad. Six months or two years.

He had a lot going for him at home in Greenly, Arkansas. A steady girlfriend, a good reputation, and a myriad of work options. The longer he was away, the greater the possibility was that some of those options would be gone when he returned. Do you take your chances with what you know or what you don't know?

Toddrick chose the unknown. Two full years of college, spent studying around the world. By the time he finished the study abroad program, he would be half way done with college.

He came to the decision on his own, but there were two people he considered the most. He'd be able to come home at the end of every semester and for holidays for a week or two, but time and distance away from those you love can be difficult. Toddrick knew that.

Life-long sweethearts are a rare occurrence in any day, but especially in the twenty-first century. Toddrick and Lisa started going steady at the age of sixteen, during the final months of their sophomore year in high school.

They were involved in each other's lives, held hands, and kissed often. Both those kids, though incredibly fond of each other, had a maturity and sensibility that put clear lines between themselves and sex. Toddrick was careful. Much more careful than I would have been. Definitely his mother's son.

True respect, friendship, and love. Very rare and very romantic. Fun to watch.

Graduation meant a parting of ways for Toddrick and Lisa. He was leaving for two years on a study abroad program. However, it's not like they would be out of range. In this technological world, no one is farther away then a phone call or a text message. Web cams and the internet keep people connected, no matter how far apart they are.

I don't think Lisa knew what she was going to do after graduation. She was smart and able-minded, well-rounded and supported by Mom and Dad's fat check book. For her, there was no limit.

Now I'm not in anybody's mind or heart, but I've watched Toddrick since he was born. I think he decided long ago that he loved Lisa Bedford and that he was going to marry her. If that was the case, he was taking an awful big risk in leaving.

Love doesn't always last time and distance. Especially when you're eighteen and the world is at your feet.

The night before Toddrick left for New York, the first stop on his educational tour, he and Lisa went on one last date. After dinner at a little café, they walked through the local WWII museum. It was toward the later part of the evening and most shops where closing. There was still a bit of foot traffic on the streets, but mostly from people walking to their cars as the town square was shutting down.

Toddrick held her hand as they strolled at a snail's pace. The longer they took to get to the car, the longer the night would be.

"So," he said. "I'm off tomorrow for a long time." She didn't say anything. "Kind of exciting, right?"

She smiled but didn't look at him. "Exciting for some of us." She laughed a little. Both the smile and the laugh were fake.

Toddrick knew Lisa well enough to detect her subtle sarcasm. "Since I'll be gone so long," he was using his own sarcastic tone, "I think I need to fill up my canteen."

She looked at him, dumbfounded. "What? Canteen?"

"Yep," Toddrick said. "Since I won't get any loving from you for a while, I need to fill up my canteen to keep me whole while we're apart." He puckered his lips. "We should probably start kissing."

Her smile dissolved. "You're weird." She let go of his hand and wrapped her arms around her waist. "And I don't want to fill up your canteen. Why don't you just stay here and I'll top it off every day?" They walked again in silence before she added, "I'm going to need to get a real job." She stepped away from him. "And there isn't a college that would turn down my dad's money." Lisa raised her eyebrows. "I could be gone faster than anyone. Never to be heard from again."

She'd been a waitress for years. It was a job she did because she was responsible, not because she needed the money. And she always claimed that waitresses worked harder than anyone else. When she'd told her father she'd gotten a job as a waitress, it was he who declared, "Waitress! Shouldn't you get a real job . . . a job you can make a career out of? It's never too early to start." Since then she always joked that she didn't have a real job.

"Yep," she said. "You're going away, and I am too." She sounded like she was threatening him.

"I know," Toddrick interjected excitedly. "Harvard, right? That's exciting."

"Or," she enunciated, acting like she'd been interrupted. "I could be a wife." She hesitated, "And a mom."

Toddrick tripped over his feet. His eyes widened and his smile looked off-centered. He regained his composure and wiped the smirk off his face. He put one arm around her shoulder, and she leaned into his chest. "Two years is a long time to wait for something," he said. "Especially when you already know what you want."

"Don't you know what you want?" she asked, pleading in her voice. "Can't we go to college together? I'll go here with you."

He looked up at the sky, like there was an answer in the stars. Warm summer nights in the South are wonderful. The stars to sky ratio is perfect, and the temperature allows you to be without a jacket at all times. I know how easy it is to let the perfect Southern nights lull you into false security. You would almost say yes to anything at that time of the night, just to keep everyone happy. You would say yes to a snake bite before you turned your back on a warm Southern night.

"I know some things I want," he said. "But I have to make sure I'm ready. I want to know what's out there. I can't really choose if I don't know all the options." He tugged her hand and pulled her forward. "I want to be good. Good for my family."

"You are good," she said. "You're the best person I know."

"I'm not. There's a lot I haven't seen. My dad would want me to be stronger and wiser. I'm just a kid." He shook his head. "Kids shouldn't be husbands or dads."

Lisa looked annoyed. "Well, you have to be sure about something."

Toddrick kissed her softly. "I know I want you. I always have." He looked pained, not the way I thought he should after a kiss.

Lisa kissed him back. "Isn't that enough?"

"*You* are definitely enough."

"Then what's the matter?"

"I've got to go do this. For us." He kissed her again. "I love you."

"Then stay here with me. You don't have to go." Lisa looked hopeful. "I don't think I love you. I know I do."

Alas, something more important than Lisa called to Toddrick. He left the next day and broke her heart. A lot of relationships end in similar ways. Life can pull people in different directions. Sometimes it works out, other times it doesn't. There is no eternal law that states you'll get what you want and the person you love will love you back.

I truly believe that Toddrick thought life would wait for him while he was away from those he loved. He was smart, but still a kid. Maybe if he'd known what was going to happen, he would have stayed. Oh, to see the future before it comes.

When Toddrick returned home for good, his world and those he'd left behind had changed.

CHAPTER FOURTEEN

To say that Jimmy struggled was an understatement. The choices laid at his feet where very similar to those laid at Toddrick's, or any other young man of their age. Jimmy, however, took his traditional path: the hard one.

I watched him, and I hurt with him.

Something fueled Jimmy that was difficult for me to detect. He seemed off. Like a hunting rifle scope that showed a target, but when you pulled the trigger, the bullet would go in a course not predicted. Jimmy was a bullet that could not be aimed.

I thought he was angry all the time. I often thought his behavior was revenge on someone or something.

As a father, it was hard to witness.

At school, his behavior deteriorated rapidly. He almost didn't graduate. A few times, he had some brushes with the law. He had a problem with arbitrary rules that existed for administrative purposes, and he didn't respond well to those who enforced them. He moved out of his family home and into a one-bedroom apartment nearby, close enough to visit his mother and receive aid when necessary, but far enough to make his own rules.

I couldn't help but see the little boy on the soccer field who refused to play by the rules. He wasn't bad, but he didn't respond to the status quo. On more than one occasion, jail time was required.

It was usually small things that compounded on top of each other and until they became big things. Like speeding tickets that never got paid, or court dates that were ignored. He was found in contempt of court for failure to pay his fines and several failures to appear.

If it were me, I'd pay the fine, slow down, and show up to my appointments. Anybody would. For Jimmy, it was all out war against the speed limit and those who enforced it.

He created a name for himself among the deputies of the area. Pulling Jimmy over for speeding was a game they would play. Jimmy knew them well, and they him.

Jimmy claimed the deputies ignored the speed limit while they were both on and off duty. He had no qualms with voicing the hypocritical nature of their behavior. He articulated it well. Lord knows he had plenty of practice talking to the deputies about it. It appeared to him that because they wore a badge and enforced traffic laws, they considered themselves exempt from honoring the law.

Most of us get a speeding ticket in our life. Or two or ten. We deal with it and go on. Not Jimmy.

He'd been in jail for two nights and was waiting inside the courtroom to address the judge.

Toddrick arrived home only hours before Jimmy's court appearance. Jimmy never wanted Summer there, didn't want his mother to see his demise, but he didn't know Toddrick was back. Summer sent Toddrick straight to the courtroom to be here eyes and ears. He slipped into the back, unnoticed by Jimmy.

Jimmy's left eye was swollen and blackened around the edges. The left side of his mouth was a puffy and pink, raw-looking. The cheek on the same side of his face was cut in several places, dry blood already showing scabs. On his way to the bar, he looked at a woman who sat near the front of the public seating area. She held a pen and paper in her hands. He winked at her, a strangely flirtatious move for a man in handcuffs.

The judge looked down from the bench. He removed his spectacles and feathered through some papers. "Good morning, Jimmy," he said without looking up. Judge Paxton had seen Jimmy in his courtroom so many times that he addressed him like they were old friends. Only there was a bite in Paxton's voice that made it clear they weren't really friends at all. "I'd like to say I'm surprised to see you again, but I'm not." He arranged the papers in his hands in a perfectly symmetrical stack and set it down.

Jimmy smiled and then winced in pain. The upward curve of his mouth cracked open a cut on his lip, and blood leaked down his chin. He wiped the blood with the back of his hands, which were still cuffed. "Good morning, you're Honor."

Paxton took his glasses off and examined Jimmy's face. "You're here for the usual, right?" Jimmy nodded, and Paxton crinkled his forehead. "Then why are you all bruised up? You didn't struggle when they took you into custody, did you?"

"No, sir. This what happens when you don't struggle." He pointed to his head. "I'd probably be buried in the ground somewhere with a few bullets in my back if I'd *struggled*."

The judge snorted. "Oh, come on. You don't expect me to believe that you were peacefully apprehended and this happened?" He pointed with the edge of his glasses to Jimmy's face.

Jimmy smiled. This time he ignored the split lip, and a drop of blood appeared. "I'm a lot of things, Your Honor. But I'm not a liar. You know me good, Judge. You ever know me to lie?" There was a moment of silence in the room. "These," he pointed to his face, "were thoughtfully given to me after my hands were cuffed." Jimmy looked over his shoulder and scanned the room. His eyes stopped on a deputy in a dark blue uniform. A round-brimmed hat rested on top his head. The deputy's hands were clasped around his belly. "That deputy," Jimmy said.

Voices in the courtroom murmured. Paxton slammed his gavel against his desk.

"Order! Order!"

The woman on the front row was frantically writing on her paper. The judge looked threateningly at the deputy before flipping through the papers again. He pulled one out of the stack and looked at it.

"It says here that you've refused the right to counsel." Paxton rolled his eyes at Jimmy. "I assume you will be representing yourself, like last time?"

"No offense, Judge." Jimmy eyed the row of attorneys sitting in their usual spot. "Those guys and their language is part of this system's problem. They have to honor *administrative* rules. They can't say certain words; they have to know cases and examples, blah, blah, blah. They are so smart, but they're simultaneously dumb because they can only say so much. They have to walk in the guidelines of their muddied-up profession. I know what I gotta say and I know how I gotta say it."

"What?" Judge Paxton scribbled on some papers, dividing his attention between the paperwork and Jimmy. "What do you have to say?" It looked like he'd already made his decision. Perhaps he had filled out the same paperwork for Jimmy so many times that he just thought he should get started on it.

While Paxton was looking at his paper work, Jimmy shot a glance at the woman with the pencil and paper. She was scribbling furiously, but he winked at her when she looked up. She put her pencil down, took out her cell phone, and placed it on the bench in front of her. She pressed a button and then continued to scribble on the note pad.

"What do you have to say, son?" Paxton repeated.

Jimmy suppressed a smile. "How fast did you drive to work today?"

"What?" Paxton looked confused. "Are you asking me?"

"I'm asking you," Jimmy said kindly. He repeated the question. "How fast did you drive to work today?"

The judge rolled his eyes. "I have no idea."

"Why don't you know? You drive the speed limit, don't you? If you do, you would probably know how fast you were going. Were you going the speed limit?"

Paxton's face turned pink. He put down his pen and folded his hands on top of his desk. He looked at the public seating area and, for the first time, he noticed the woman frantically writing on the pad of paper. He also noticed the cell phone that lay in front of her. For a second, she and the judge met eyes, and she realized the attention she'd drawn to herself. Casually, she put a strand of hair behind her ear, picked the phone up, and stowed it out of sight.

"I assume I drove the speed limit," Paxton said. "I didn't get pulled over." Several people in the room laughed. "Why does it matter? I'm not in trouble for speeding." He pointed at Jimmy. "You are."

"I'm here because I was speeding," Jimmy said. "I know that." He could tell the judge was losing his patience. And when the judge loses patience, it usually means an immediate ruling. When the judge gives a ruling while he's upset, it ends up being bad for the person who caused the foul mood. Jimmy could sense that it was coming. He put his hands up like he was surrendering. "Hear me out. Follow me for just a minute, and I'll show you why it's important."

Paxton eyed the courtroom. All eyes were on him. He motioned for Jimmy to continue.

"Do you know what the speed limit is on your street?" Jimmy's question was simple.

Paxton looked like he regretted giving Jimmy the opportunity to ask the question. "I think it's thirty-five miles an hour on my street, and the limit increases to fifty when I get on Tyson Parkway." He smiled. "From there, it's all highway."

Jimmy tried unsuccessfully to hide his smile. "The posted speed limit on your street is twenty-five miles an hour, and on Don Tyson it switches to forty-five. Do you know how fast you drive to Don Tyson every morning?"

"Jimmy, I'm guessing that you know how fast I drive." Paxton eyed the woman on the front row. She was looking at him, waiting for him to respond. "You tell me. Am I within the limit?"

Jimmy scratched his head. "I'm glad you asked. Last

month I bought a radar gun off Ebay. It's old, but it works. I've spent the past three weeks following you and your deputies." Jimmy's smile was as big as it could be. "Almost every day you drive forty miles an hour in a twenty-five mile speed zone. When you hit Tyson Parkway, you often get up to seventy miles an hour in a forty-five."

The courtroom gasped.

"I don't blame you for going over the speed limit," Jimmy continued. "I said I followed your deputies too. I've got over a hundred videos on my phone of your deputies ignoring the speed limit at almost every hour of the day. Off and on duty. I've got videos of them all over the county. From here all the way to Spook Lake, you and your deputies driving over a hundred miles an hour sometimes."

"You have video of me driving from my house to Spook Lake," Paxton repeated.

Jimmy nodded. "On my phone."

Paxton cleared his throat. "What's your point, son?" The judge was out of patience.

"The point is, your honor, well... what's the difference between me breaking the speed limit and you or the deputies breaking the speed limit? Or me and the millions of people who drive faster than the speed limit every day?

The judge waved his hands in exasperation. "I don't know. Does it even matter?"

"I get caught. Does that sound fair to you? Does that sound just? Thousands of people speed in this city every day, your employees included . . . you included."

"You have footage?" the judge stated.

"Can you read the notes on the bottom of my ticket? It

should tell you how far over the speed limit I was going."

The judge put his spectacles back on. He looked at the cardstock slip that was Jimmy's ticket receipt. "Going thirty in a twenty," Paxton read aloud. "Jimmy! I don't care how far over the speed limit you were going. You are here because you didn't pay your fines and a warrant was issued for your arrest. What don't you get about that?"

"I know, your Honor. This is me trying to defend myself." He cleared his throat. "What if it was actually only four miles over and the officer decided to round up? What if I was driving three, or even two over the limit? Who's gonna check? It's just his word against mine."

Jimmy wasn't trying to say he wasn't guilty; he was trying to say that everyone was guilty of the same infraction, but that some people pay for it and others don't.

I told you I'm a simple man. If I got a ticket, I paid it and forgot about it. I didn't think the argument was going to work out in Jimmy's favor, but I had to give him credit for trying. By pointing out the inconsistencies in the general observance of the speed limit, I think he was hoping to get himself out of trouble. How can you hold some people accountable for breaking the speed limit while other people don't have to observe it?

"Judge," Jimmy continued. "You might not like what I'm about to say, but I'm gonna say it anyway. The deputy who pulled me over knew I was coming and planned to pull me over whether I was speeding or not, which I wasn't. I don't always go the speed limit, but this time I was."

Jimmy's expression changed from cool and collected to angry. "He's been following me, off and on, for a few days. He needed a reason to pull me over, and speeding was what he chose. It's easy to make that one up. If you run the footage on the stop, you'll see." Jimmy scoffed. "What's ironic is that I have footage of Strein breaking the speed limit day after day. Almost every hour of every day. Hypocrite," Jimmy spat.

"Deputy Strein." Judge Paxton read the deputy's name off the ticket. The judge waved his hand for the deputy to approach the stand.

The deputy's shoulders were broad and his stomach thick. He looked strong. He removed his black-brimmed hat as he approached the bench. The judge waved Jimmy forward until both he and the deputy were standing side by side in front of the judge's desk. The tension between the two could be felt by all in the room, like when you're outside and the storm clouds are overhead and the wind is picking up. You know a storm is coming. You feel it in the air.

There was a storm brewing between Strein and Jimmy.

"Deputy Strein," the judge asked, "did you pull the defendant over for speeding?"

"Yes." There was no hesitation in Strein's voice.

"How fast was he speeding?" Paxton asked.

"As the document says, Your Honor. Five miles over the speed limit."

The judge looked at Jimmy. "I don't know what to tell you, son. You were speeding."

Jimmy smiled. "Judge, seeing as how I'm representing myself, can I ask the *honest* deputy a few questions?"

"Do you mind?" Paxton asked Strein. "I want him out of this courtroom as fast as possible."

Strein shrugged his shoulders. "I don't care."

"Thank you, Your Honor." Jimmy turned to the deputy. "Deputy Strein. What is the address of your girlfriend?"

Strein's face turned red.

"You don't have to answer that," the judge said. "Young man," he said pointedly to Jimmy, "this session is over."

"Okay, Okay." Jimmy backpeddled. "You'll see where I'm going. I'll ask the same question in a different way." Before he could get a yes or no from the judge, he said, "If you'll look at the address and street where the," Jimmy made quotation marks with his fingers, "'traffic violation' was made, it will read that it took place somewhere on Carnation Drive." He turned to face the deputy. "Do you know anybody who lives on Carnation Drive?"

The deputy held a straight face. No response.

"Okay, he pleads the fifth on that, but how about this one." Jimmy addressed the deputy again. "Deputy Strein, you seem like a strong, strapping man. I'd say that when most criminals see you, they don't try anything because they're scared to. You're intimidating. You can take care of yourself, right? A guy would have to be out of his mind to pull something over on you on account of the beating he'd take."

The deputy's eyes cut into Jimmy like knives into butter.

Jimmy's voice turned sarcastic. "Being as strong and mighty as you are, can you tell me how someone like me can be a threat?"

"That's it, Jimmy. We are done here." Paxton pointed at the bailiff. "Remove Jimmy from the courtroom."

Jimmy raised his voice, making sure all in the room

could hear. "That deputy falsely pulled me over because I was kissing his girlfriend. She lives on Carnation Drive, and I was leaving there when the bogus traffic violation occurred. He handcuffed me and beat the tar out of me all while I was in handcuffs."

The bailiff grabbed Jimmy by the arm and started dragging him to the closest exit. Jimmy dragged his feet. "I'll sue you," he shouted, pointing his head at the deputy. "And I'll sue you," he pointed at the judge, "and I won't use one of these pencil-neck paper pushers; stupid, weak attorneys. I'll get one of the big ones who'll destroy you guys."

The judge smashed his gavel on top of his desk. "Bailiff, put him in my chambers. Strein," Paxton pointed at the deputy, who was already walking toward the nearest exit, "you too. My chambers, now!"

CHAPTER FIFTEEN

Paxton's chambers were small, not like the ones you see in the movies. No polished wood or mahogany surroundings. Normal desks with office furniture and shelves full of used and never-read books. Papers were cluttered on top of the desk with a large stack of manila folders. In the corner by the door, a few burlap bags were stacked against the wall. Small swirls of white powder were visible around the bags. It looked like debris from a work site had been piled in the corner of the office.

Paxton sat in the imitation leather chair behind his desk and folded his arms across his midsection. Jimmy and Deputy Strein occupied two of the four chairs in the room.

"I don't know what to do with you," Paxton said, looking at Jimmy. "I know the law isn't perfect, and I know you can't hold everyone accountable to the law all the time." He slammed his fist down on the desk. "But you've been in my courtroom too many times. There are bigger problems in this county, and I'm tired of you making a bigger fuss than what you're worth."

He looked at Strein, his eyes pulsating like they were about to pop. "And you. You could go to jail for this. I'm guessing you *did* hit him while he was handcuffed." Paxton rubbed his temples with his hands. "You are suspended, and an investigation will be launched against you as it regards to this situation."

"Judge," Strein began, but Paxton cut him off.

"If I find out that he was kissing your girl and you did this," he pointed at Jimmy's face, "you will be in serious trouble."

"I don't have to listen to this." Strein stood up from his chair.

"Sit down!" the judge ordered. "We have to flush this ou. I don't want to be in this situation again. I mean it," he boomed, looking at Jimmy. "I'm tired of seeing you in my courtroom. Now," he said with more control in his voice, "why are you recording the police while they drive, and why on earth do you have a speed gun?"

"I just don't like double standards. I'm tired of getting pulled over for doing what everyone else is doing," Jimmy answered. "Including you and him."

Paxton sighed, a deep and relenting sound that indicated he was going to surrender. "We all hate double standards, kid." There was genuine compassion in Paxton's voice. "Strein, you can go, but you and I aren't finished." Paxton's tone turned rough again. "Until we can meet with your sergeant about this, you best be quiet as a mouse. Is that clear?"

"Yes, sir," Strein said, noncommittally. He left the room without another word.

Jimmy squirmed in his chair as Paxton stared at him.

"Who was that in the courtroom jotting down notes?

Was she recording the conversation?"

"My friend," Jimmy admitted. "Norma works for the Daily Southern. She's been helping me with my speed gun. It seemed good to have someone else witness what I was seeing. I wanted to prove that everyone speeds, but the cops only enforce it when they want to or when it's convenient. I'm not hurting anybody. Who decides the speed limit, anyway?"

"I get it, son. But why do you have to do this? Are you planning on running a story or something with all the videos and speed work you've done?" Paxton sounded interested.

"I'm thinking more like a documentary. Nothing is secret these days anyway, with iPhones and such. I'm not looking to hurt you or anybody. I just want to be left alone." Jimmy fell silent, letting the implications of what he was saying sink in. "I guess if you drop all charges against me, have that idiot Strein on some kind of discipline, hopefully fired," he mumbled, "I'll reconsider. I'd hate to see this story get on the news and ruin a re-election campaign."

"Good lord, Jimmy. That's blackmail."

Jimmy looked incredulous. "I'm not blackmailing anybody. I just want equal treatment. If the rest of the driving populace doesn't get a ticket, I don't get one either. If you don't get a ticket, I don't."

Someone knocked on the door. It opened a few inches, and a head appeared.

"Judge Paxton, may I come in?" Toddrick smiled, showing his teeth.

"Toddrick! Come on in." Jimmy spoke like the office belonged to him. He walked to Toddrick, gave him a strong hug, and pulled him through the doorway. "Sit down." He pointed at the chair next to his. "Judge Paxton and I were just about finished."

Toddrick sat down in the chair and looked at Paxton, whose mood seemed to have gotten better.

"Hi, Toddrick. Back from school?"

"Yes. All that abroad nonsense has made me miss this backwoods place really bad." Toddrick crossed his legs and leaned back in the chair.

"Well, if you go again, take this hoodlum with you." Paxton pointed at Jimmy. "Seriously, talk some sense into him. He's running amuck of his life and my deputies. It isn't good. Look at his face. One of my deputies beat him while he was in handcuffs. I'd like to take Jimmy's side, but something tells me he had it coming."

Jimmy nodded. "I'm with you on that, Judge. I *was* kissing his girlfriend. Kind of a lot." Jimmy laughed, but he was the only one. He looked from the judge to Toddrick, and neither one of them saw the humor. Jimmy cleared his throat. "I was tired of him following me. I wanted to get back at him. Mess with him a little."

"See what I mean?" Paxton said.

"Well, I'll be around for good now. Jimmy and I will be hanging out together all the time." Toddrick looked at Jimmy. "Just like old times."

"You do that, please. Now, get out of my office. Both of you. I have to return to my courtroom. My courtroom." He looked at Jimmy and pointed at his chest. "My courtroom," he repeated. "Get that woman, Norma, out of my courtroom. I hate feeling like I'm being watched."

"Bail?" Toddrick asked. "Can I post it for Jimmy?"

Paxton eyed Jimmy. "No bail. Jimmy's gone through enough this go around. Now get out of my office."

Once they were outside the courthouse, Toddrick started to laugh. "Kissing another man's girlfriend! Really? Problems with the ladies?"

Jimmy joined in the laughter. "You have no idea, but you shouldn't be teasing me about having problems with the ladies. I'm sure you'll be coming to me for advice soon enough."

Toddrick stopped laughing. "What are you talking about?"

"Nothing, really, but I need to get my phone. You have to take me to Strein's girlfriend's house. I left if there the night I got arrested."

Toddrick shook his head. "I'm not taking you to her house. I'm staying away from everything connected to that deputy." Toddrick turned serious, all mirth out of his face. "Hey, what did you mean, just now . . . that I'll be coming to you for advice?"

"I heard about Lisa's engagement. Pretty crazy, right?" Jimmy laughed again, but stopped when Toddrick didn't join in. "Wait, you didn't know?"

CHAPTER SIXTEEN

Toddrick's step faltered. Judging by the look on his face, Lisa hadn't told him anything.

"Oh, Toddrick," Jimmy said. "Haven't you been talking to her? I think she's been engaged for a couple months. You should've been the first person to know."

"I have been talking to her." Toddrick put a finger to his mouth and looked at the ground, like he was thinking. "Well, I guess I've been texting her off and on." He started to walk again, but slowly. "Maybe it's been longer than I thought. Does she still work at the diner? I'm starving. Maybe we could grab a bite to eat and see her. Two birds with one stone."

Jimmy raised an eyebrow. "Shouldn't you know where she works?"

Toddrick pushed Jimmy toward the car. "Let's just get out of here."

"Hey," Jimmy said. "You drove Mom's car?"

"Yes. I spent the morning with her. I would have taken yours, but Strein had it towed. You'll need to get it later. Now get in the car. I need to eat."

At the diner, Toddrick flagged down a waitress and asked where Lisa was.

"I don't know. She stopped working here months ago." She pursed her lips together, reconsidering. "No, wait; it's been at least a year." The waitress shook her head. "Wow. Time flies."

Toddrick looked dumbfounded. Jimmy continued the conversation with the waitress while Toddrick looked at everything and nothing, his eyes were far away.

"Do you know where she works now?" Jimmy asked.

"She works at Johnson and Shackley." She pointed before she walked off. "Just down the road."

"A law firm?" Toddrick crinkled his nose. "She never told me she got a new job."

They walked up the sidewalk to the all-glass building. Big, white, bold letters read "Johnson and Shackley" several feet above the entrance. Toddrick got close to the window and pressed his face to the glass.

"I see her. I think she's the receptionist. She's messing around with some papers or something."

"She can probably see you. Go talk to her," Jimmy urged.

Toddrick inhaled through his nose and exhaled through his mouth like he was preparing himself to jump off a cliff. "Okay. I'm going in."

The large oval desk had a golden-flecked marble counter top. It looked sturdy and expensive. He put both hands on it and, when she didn't look up, he cleared his throat. He was only feet away from her, but she still didn't look up.

"Lisa?"

She lifted her head. Her eyes scanned his face, and their eyes met. Her mouth slowly opening.

"Hi." Toddrick smiled. "Remember me?"

She dropped the papers she was holding and wrapped her arms around her waist. Something reflected light on the wall next to her. The reflection was so large and colorful that it was hard to ignore. Toddrick's eyes followed the reflective spark to the diamond hanging on Lisa's finger. She was definitely engaged.

He stared at the ring, mouth agape. She followed his stare to her hands. When she realized what he was looking at, she quickly moved her hands behind her back.

"Wow," she said, finally saying something. "Toddrick. What a surprise. I wasn't sure if we'd ever see you again." Her tone was pleasant, but I detected the smallest hint of accusation.

Having been forced to take his eyes off the ring, he looked up at her. "I'm done. I'm back from study abroad." He swallowed. "Um, I'm back for good."

"Back for good," Lisa repeated. Her expression was closed, beautiful eyes large and emotionless. She wasn't letting anything get inside her mind. "That's nice. I bet your family is happy."

They stood silent for a few seconds, but it felt like several minutes. "

What's his name?" Toddrick asked.

"Who? Oh." She pulled her hands from behind her back. She smiled at the ring. "Tad. His name is Tad Shackley."

Jimmy's head popped up from below the counter. He'd snuck in without either of them noticing. "Tad," Jimmy repeated. He looked like he'd eaten something he didn't like, his nose wrinkly and his eye lids almost closed.

Lisa jumped at Jimmy's appearance. She put a hand

over her mouth to cover any outburst.

"Tad, like tadpole?" Jimmy asked. "That's an odd name."

Toddrick rolled his eyes. "Can you give us a few minutes, Jimmy? Alone."

"You bet." Jimmy winked. "I don't think Tad would like that, but I'm not on his team," he whispered.

Toddrick motioned with his head toward the door, an invitation for Jimmy to leave. "Just a few minutes, please."

Lisa examined the bruises and cuts on Jimmy's face. "What happened to you?"

Without turning around, Jimmy yelled, "I kissed another man's girl. That's a warning, bro."

Lisa started to laugh. "Okay." She shook her head.

"Jimmy told me you're engaged." Toddrick was eager to carry on their conversation. "How long has it been?" His voice was cool and collected, but it lacked its normal gusto. His voice was a balloon that was slowly losing air.

"About a month." A strand of hair fell in front of her face. She moved it away and changed the subject. "Are you excited to be back? Summer break! That sounds fun."

"Yep. Fun." Toddrick looked like he was considering something, and suddenly his countenance changed. His eyes lost their dullness, and his normal spark returned. "Yikes. Where are my manners? Congratulations! Come here and give me a hug." He motioned for her to come out from behind the desk."

Lisa's tepid smile firmed up and became genuine. The tension in the air lessened, and the awkwardness dispelled. She met Toddrick on the opposite side of the desk, and he wrapped his arms around her, squeezing her in a quick but strong hug. He pulled away from her.

"When's the big day?"

"January twenty-first. Next year."

"So long? That's almost," he did some quick counting on his fingers, "eight months away."

"Yes, well, Tad has a few business trips, and we wanted to make sure we weren't rushed. Family and schedules to consider."

"Tad looks pretty successful." Toddrick looked around the office. It was adorned with artwork and sculptures. "I'm guessing Tad is the Shackley that's printed on everything?" He held up a paper pad that had "Shackley and Johnson" printed across the top.

"Yes. He's definitely doing well when it comes to money. At least, I think." Lisa stepped back behind the counter and picked up her papers. "He takes me to the nicest restaurants and he drives a nice car. His house is really nice, too."

Toddrick's eyes widened, and he swallowed. His cheeks momentarily flashed red, but then he looked pale, like he'd seen a ghost. "Are you staying at his house?"

It was Lisa's turn to look flushed. "That's none of your business, but no. I'm still the same person I was when you left." She shrugged her shoulders. "I've learned a lot about people since I started working here, though." She shook her head disbelievingly. "It would shock you some of the things we encounter. Everyone has their issues, and the number one thing that gets people is money. You'd be surprised by the amount of fighting over money we see here."

Toddrick's eyes fell to the floor. "I don't have any money." His voice sounded like that half-filled balloon again. His eyes examined the ring on Lisa's finger. "Working at a law firm? Wow. Look at you. Are you the receptionist?"

She shook her head, and half her mouth smiled. "No. I'm an intern. Just helping out with small case work." She held the bundle of papers to her chest.

"Not surprised. You were always the smartest person I knew. That's why you're going to be the best mother."

She eyed him with a furrowed brow. "Don't you mean the best attorney?"

"If you want to be that, sure. But I meant the best mother. The smarter you are, the better mother you'll be. Smart moms are so important for kids. The smarter the mom, the smarter the child."

A door opened, and a man of average height and weight walked up to the desk. He grabbed a few paperclips out of a tray and smiled at Lisa. He was a tiny bit on the heavy side, not anywhere near fat, but thick and manly. His hair was neatly combed and his features pleasant.

"Good afternoon," he said to Lisa. He kissed her on the cheek and turned to Toddrick, his hand extended in greeting. "Hi. Do we have an appointment?"

"Tad," Lisa said, "this is an old friend of mine. Toddrick."

Tad's arm almost retracted from greeting and, for a split second, I thought there was leeriness in his eyes. Like he was concerned, worried or troubled about something. He recovered so fast that I thought I was imagining it. His face melted into crinkles and smile lines. A fake smile. "Toddrick!" He grabbed Toddrick's hand and shook it. "I've heard so much about you." They released hands. "Um, back from school?"

"Yes," Toddrick answered. "Back from school and looking for a job, I guess."

"Oh?" Tad sized him up. "Well, I have a few positions opening up here. After the wedding in January," Tad stepped next to Lisa and put an arm around her waist, "there will probably be an intern position available. I'll need someone to replace Lisa. I don't know what your career objectives are, but it's good work and honest pay."

"Is that such a thing for a lawyer?" Toddrick laughed. "Honest pay, right?" He looked back and forth between Lisa and Tad, waiting for them to join in. When they didn't, he stopped and cleared his throat.

Tad leaned over and pecked Lisa on the cheek. "If you're interested in the honest work for honest pay, ask Lisa for an application. Hiring good help these days is hard. Kids just want to be on their phones, on Facebook, watching movies or playing games." He walked back to the door he'd come from. "Hopefully we'll see you again." Tad winked at Lisa. "See you tonight." He disappeared.

"Hey! He is super cool. You did good." Toddrick looked at her slyly. "How old is he? He isn't robbing the cradle, I hope." Tad did look more mature, even older than I'd expected.

"For your information, I'm almost twenty-three." She put her nose in the air in mock offense. "And he is twenty-nine."

"I'm just teasing," Toddrick said through a toothy grin. He looked closely at her face, examined her eyes with his. I'm not sure what he was doing, but I got the impression that he was looking to find something that was lost. She turned away from his gaze, so he stopped searching, or maybe he discovered that what he was looking for was no longer there. He breathed deeply and exhaled. "It's great to see you again. Hopefully I'll see you around."

"Wait." Lisa walked across the lobby and extended a few papers to him. "Here. It's an application for one of our job openings. Just menial work for now, but Tad's right. It's good work."

Toddrick looked at her, and then at the papers she was holding out to him. He didn't reach for them. "Thanks, but no." He looked out the already opened door. Jimmy was sitting on the hood of the car, eating an apple. "I'm going to work with Jimmy over the summer. I need to get to know him again."

Lisa peered out the window at Jimmy. "Does he have a job?"

"I have no idea." Toddrick let go of the door, leaving Lisa holding it ajar.

"Toddrick," she said softly.

He stopped walking and turned around. He raised his eyebrows, and indicating that he was waiting for her to speak.

"We should talk."

He winked. "We just did. I'm really happy for you."

CHAPTER SEVENTEEN

"Get a job!" Jimmy sounded insulted. "What for?"

Toddrick reached into his suitcase and started to pull out his clothes. "Everybody needs to work. Don't tell me Mom's still paying your bills."

"Says the guy who's moving back into his mother's house." Jimmy lay on the floor, throwing a football in the air. It would spiral up until it nearly hit the ceiling, and then he would wait until it almost hit his face before he snatched it out of the air. "Besides, what bills?"

Toddrick paused in the middle of putting his shirt on a hanger. "You know what, you're right. I think I'll move in with you instead. Easier to keep an eye on you."

He took his shirt off the hanger as Jimmy's mouth opened in protest.

"I didn't mean--" Jimmy began, but Toddrick held up a hand.

"I accept your invite. It'll be great fun. You and I are going to get jobs and work together until school starts this fall." He looked at Jimmy with "prepare-yourself" eyes. "And you're going to college. Being abroad has shown me tons, but mostly that I hardly know anything . . . or anybody. There are a lot of things out there, and five times as many people as there are things. You have to go to school."

"I'm not doing anything." Jimmy threw the ball at Toddrick. Quick with his hands, he caught it just before it smashed into his nose. He threw it back at Jimmy, and it buried itself in his stomach, making him to moan.

"And," Toddrick continued, his voice playful, "we need to keep you away from the police. Do you really have a radar gun?" He snorted.

Jimmy sat up, his eyes intense now. "Absolutely. It's pretty cool. I love catching those hypocrite police breaking their own rules." He set the football on the floor. "I have a log of the times and places I watched them. Their most popular place for speeding? Right outside the sheriff's office." He rolled his eyes. "Ironic, huh?"

Toddrick laughed. "Yep. We *have* to get you a job."

"You should be focusing on your problem, brother." Jimmy moved from the floor to the bed. He lay down and crossed his legs.

"My problem?"

"Yeah. Lisa getting married?" Jimmy was effective at turning the conversation. "I can't believe you didn't know."

Even though he was teasing, Jimmy's comment obviously struck a sore spot. Toddrick's optimism faltered, and his enthusiasm in the conversation diminished. He closed his suitcase and sat down on the bed, his eyes vacant.

"It's my fault. I should have done more. I was just

focusing on school." Toddrick looked at Jimmy, a little moisture in his eyes. "I screwed that up. Man, Tad is pretty cool."

Jimmy twisted his face. "I was just kidding. Don't worry about Lisa. There are plenty of fish in the sea. Hey! I know. You can follow my example and start kissing other people's girlfriends. It makes life very exciting." He raised his eyebrows a few times and grinned crookedly.

Toddrick stuck his tongue out like he had a bad taste in his mouth. "Why would I want to kiss a girl who has a boyfriend? Any girl who would do that isn't my kind of girl."

"Whatever. You want to kiss a girl who is about to get married. Don't you? What's the difference?"

Toddrick nodded. "Sure, but she's Lisa. She was my girl. And Lisa isn't that way."

"What way?" Jimmy sounded like he was getting offended.

"You know what I mean. She isn't the type to suck face with people just because they're hot or attractive. I think she's loyal. That's why I love—" he stopped himself from saying it. He did love her, but I think he knew he'd only be hurting himself if he professed his love. Instead of saying it, he grunted. "It's my fault."

Jimmy pushed himself off the bed. "You know what you need? A welcome home celebration. Just you and me and some good food and drinks." He looked at the time on his phone. "And it's getting to be past dinner time. Let's go get some ribs. Smokin' Joes?"

"A bar? Man, what happened to you?"

"Cool your jets, it's not for the beer. It's for the ribs." He winked. "And the girls."

"Girls hang out at bars?" Toddrick shot him a sideways glare. "Hopefully you're looking for someone more responsible. Or are we still sixteen?"

"Whatever. I'm starving. Let's get some food."

***

Jimmy finished the last bite of ribs and put a dry bone back on his plate. "If you're really looking for a summer job, go down to the rice plant. I hear it's a good wage, and they're always hiring. I'll work with you through the summer, but that's it. I'd like to buy a new car."

"Sell your radar gun." Toddrick cleaned his fingers with a napkin. "You're going to enroll in school with me this fall, and tuition is expensive. You'll need the money."

Noise near the front of the bar drew their attention. The raised voices and ruckus was difficult to ignore.

"Let me in," a male voice yelled. "I know he's in there."

Jimmy spotted the guy yelling and smiled. "I thought I recognized that voice." He raised his cup and took a drink. "Be ready for a fight," he warned.

"What?" Toddrick looked to the commotion and tried to see what Jimmy meant.

"Yep." Jimmy looked excited. "Hopefully he brought friends. He's gonna need 'em."

"Who?"

"Strein." Jimmy slouched in his chair, making himself look as comfortable as possible. "I'm not in handcuffs this time."

The sound of glass shattering and chairs skidding on wood gathered the attention of every person in the bar. All heads turned towards the clatter, except Jimmy's. He looked in the opposite direction, his expression coy.

"Toddrick," Jimmy said coolly. "I'm gonna let him hit

me, so don't do anything. After that, it becomes self-defense. Got it?"

Toddrick shook his head. "You're ridiculous."

Strein approached the table, a brown bottle half full of sloshing liquid in his hands. Fresh blood ran on his knuckles, a result of whatever he'd done to get through the doors.

"Call the police," the bartender told a waitress. She pulled the phone off the wall and dialed.

"Good evening, Deputy Strein. Care to join us?" Jimmy pointed to a vacant chair next to the table.

Strein put the bottle to his lips and took loud gulps. He wiped away a few drops from the corners of his mouth. "Not deputy. Not anymore." He took another drink. Clearly, he was drunk. When he talked, his words were slurred and wet, drenched with booze. He reeked of liquor and swayed from side to side. It looked like he was on a ship at sea, moving up and down with the waves. Or maybe a tree that was swaying with the breeze, except there was no breeze.

"They fired me because of that." He pointed to Jimmy's bruised eye. "It's frowned upon in my line of work." He took another drink. "Hitting people."

Jimmy's face was attentive, like he was listening with great interest. "What about this?" He pointed to his split lip. "Oh, and I have a few bruises on my ribs." He lifted up his shirt, exposing black and blue marks on his midsection. "Are those frowned on too?"

Strein ignored him. "I've come to finish the job." He let out a tiny belch. "It's my last task."

Jimmy sniffed loudly. He waved his hand in front of his face like he was trying to clear the air. "You are definitely drunk." He leaned over to Toddrick and whispered, "This is going to be easier than I thought." He cleared his throat and looked back a Strein. "How's Melissa?"

Strein threw the bottle at the ground, and it broke in pieces, sending glass and liquid debris in all directions. "Leave her out of this." He grabbed Jimmy by the shirt and pulled him out of his chair. He reared back his right fist and slammed it into Jimmy's already damaged face, sending Jimmy toppling over the table.

Surprisingly, Jimmy was on his feet a second after he hit the ground. His hands were up in a defensive boxing position. "Oh, look," he said. "No handcuffs." A trickle of blood rolled down his cheek, a new cut under his eye.

Strein flung himself at Jimmy, but Jimmy was sober, well-practiced, and, like he said—no handcuffs. He stepped to one side, dodging Strein's wild punch and landing a punch of his own.

The two men collided in a confusing skirmish. It was difficult to see which man was which and who was hitting who. Toddrick had just bent down to separate the two when blue flashing lights shown through the window. In seconds, the police had Strein and Jimmy separated and sitting on the floor.

Jimmy held his hands up. "Handcuffs again. Two times in one day. I have to admit, even that's too much for me."

A deputy approached Jimmy. "Stand up, please." Jimmy got off the ground. "Come on. Let me see the cuffs. We're letting you go."

Jimmy extended his hands. As the officer inserted the key to uncuff the links, he said, "Everyone saw Strein attack you. You were just defending yourself." Jimmy's hands fell free, and the officer asked, "Do you want to press charges?"

"Me? Press charges?" He smiled and shook his head. "Nah. He'll get what's coming to him. I just want to go home." He looked at Toddrick. "I've got to get a job and then go to college. Pssh!" His tone was full of sarcasm.

"Great," the deputy said as he walked away. "Less paperwork for me."

CHAPTER EIGHTEEN

Toddrick knocked on Jimmy's open bedroom door. "Get up. It's time to go."

Jimmy stirred in his bed.

"Let's go!" Toddrick shouted. "We need to go by the rice plant and fill out job applications."

On the other side of the apartment, someone knocked on the front door. It was a faint sound, but very recognizable.

"Someone's at the door," Toddrick said. "I'll get it, but you have to get up. And hurry."

Toddrick opened the front door, and his eyes widened in surprise. "Good morning, Deputy . . ." Toddrick read the name badge on the uniform. "Deputy Shawnston. How can I help you?" A second and third deputy emerged from behind the first. Three police cruisers were parked around the house. A little too many for just a house call.

"Is Jimmy Cook here?" the first deputy asked.

"Um, yeah. He's here." Toddrick looked concerned. "What's this about? Speeding tickets? Judge Paxton released Jimmy yesterday."

Jimmy walked into the entryway and stood next to Toddrick. He was wearing jeans, but he held his T-shirt in his hands. He pulled the shirt over his head. "Good morning, Deputy Shawnston. It's nice to see you again." His tone was sarcastic and accusatory, like he blamed the officer for the early morning wake up call. "How fast did you drive here?"

The deputy reached behind his back and pulled out a pair of handcuffs. "Jimmy Cook, you're under arrest for the murder of Jonathon Strein."

CHAPTER NINETEEN

Deaths as gruesome as John Strein's are rare. Especially around those parts. He'd been smashed in the head by the blunt end of a hammer, over and over. Forensics revealed that five times the hammer had broken clean through the skull, leaving large messy craters in Strein's head. The murder weapon was found just a few feet from the body, covered with traces of hair and caked with drying blood.

According to the paper, there were several witnesses that saw Strein and Jimmy fight the night of his death. One source also quoted Jimmy as saying, "He'll get what's coming to him." This was fact, and Toddrick knew it. He'd been there for the fight and he'd heard Jimmy say Strein would get what's coming to him.

Unfortunately, Jimmy had a documented, long and unfriendly history with Strein. He had recently been beaten by the dirty deputy, kissed his girlfriend, and they'd fought many times in public. Jimmy had articulable motive to kill Strein. At least, according to the paper.

To implicate him even further, the murder weapon had Jimmy's fingerprints all over it. When the police questioned Jimmy about that, he shrugged his shoulders and said, "Of course it has my fingerprints on it. It's my hammer, but I didn't kill him."

To make matters worse, Jimmy stuck with his preferred methodology on legal representation. He believed he could speak to his position better than anyone else. He'd often referred to lawyers as paperwork and administratively locked, pencil-necked attorneys. Consequently, he refused legal representation.

Jimmy needed help.

It was under these dire circumstances that Toddrick pushed open the glass door to Shackley and Johnston, Attorney at Law. He walked up to the familiar oval desk, but it wasn't Lisa behind the counter this time.

"Hello," the woman greeted cheerfully. "How can I help you?"

"Is Lisa here?"

"Yes. Is she expecting you?"

Toddrick shook his head. "No."

She picked up the office phone on her desk, pressed a button, and waited. "Lisa. Hi. There's a young man here who wants to see you." She paused, and then looked at Toddrick. "What's your name, sweetie?"

"Toddrick," he said cheerfully.

"Toddrick," she repeated into the receiver. "Okay, I'll send him back." She hung up the phone and directed Toddrick down the hall to the third door on the right. The door read "INTERN." He tapped it with his knuckles, and it opened immediately.

Lisa smiled sympathetically. "I'm *so sorry* about Jimmy. Come on in." She directed him to a chair, and he sat down. "This is insane. How are you with this?"

"I'm not good." Toddrick ran a hand through his hair. "I want to help him, but I don't know how. He refused his right to a lawyer."

Lisa nodded. "I heard." She shook her head disapprovingly. "That's not smart."

"Can you help him?" Toddrick said, pleading in his voice.

Lisa's eyes displayed a Rolla deck of options. "Give me a second." She got up from her chair and opened the door to her office. "Wait here." She returned with Tad Shackley behind her. "Tad, you remember Toddrick? He came by the other day, and I introduced you two."

"Of course I remember." Tad shook Toddrick's hand. "What can I do for you?

Before Toddrick could respond, Lisa addressed Tad. "In our staff meeting yesterday, we talked about the murder of Jonathon Strein." She gestured toward Toddrick. "Jimmy, the accused, is Toddrick's brother." Tad looked at Toddrick with new interest. "Toddrick wants us to help Jimmy."

Tad arched an eyebrow. "What kind of help?" He looked at Toddrick. "You want us to defend your brother?"

"I don't know," Toddrick said. "My brother isn't accepting a lawyer, and if you've read the papers, it's clear that everyone thinks he did it."

"Did he?" Tad asked.

Toddrick looked at Lisa and then back at Tad. "Jimmy says he didn't do it, and I believe him."

Tad eyed him. "You want Shackley and Johnston to represent Jimmy? For free, I'm guessing?"

Toddrick looked insulted. "We have money. But

actually I'm asking for a job. I want to work here and learn how to represent my brother."

"You think it's that easy?"

"I'm just looking for ways to help him." He stood up and put his hands in his pockets. "Sorry. Coming here was a bad idea." He backed toward the door.

"I could help," Lisa volunteered.

Toddrick stopped in the open doorway.

"All I'm doing is going over some of your old cases," she said to Tad. "Just insurance fraud and family settlements. Toddrick and Jimmy are old friends of mine." She looked at her fiancé like a puppy. "I can train Toddrick. Please?"

Tad looked at her. "Old friends," he repeated. "Yes, you should help them, but if you discover anything important, I need to know about it." He turned toward Toddrick. "I'll represent your brother, but you two do the leg work."

Lisa smiled. "Thanks, Tad!"

"Don't make me regret it, babe."

I detected hidden concern in his voice. Tad was a smart man and knew there was a history between his fiancé and Toddrick.

"Now, I've got work to do." He walked past Toddrick and stopped. "You need to fill out an official application if you're going to be an employee here."

Toddrick smiled. "Thanks, Mr. Shackley."

Tad didn't return the smile. "It doesn't pay much. But this case will be good for business. Call me Tad."

CHAPTER TWENTY

"Thanks, Lisa," Toddrick said after Tad left her office. "I was hoping you would help, but I don't think Tad was too keen on the idea. He really likes you, huh?"

"It's more than just liking me. He loves me." She pointed to her engagement ring. "Is it such a surprise that he would do favors for me?"

"No. I'm not surprised." Toddrick chewed on his lip. It looked like he wanted to say more. Instead he redirected his attention toward the task at hand. "Where do we start? Do we look for clues or something?"

"We start with Jimmy."

* * *

A thick plate of translucent plastic separated Toddrick and Lisa from Jimmy. He wore an orange jump suit and smiled at them through the barrier.

"Why are you smiling?" Toddrick asked. "You're in jail."

He shrugged his shoulders. "Honestly, I feel pretty good in here. The cops can't chase me around and give me meaningless tickets. I'm not getting handcuffed and beaten. I'm not being followed. I'm safe in here."

Lisa looked confused. "Safe? There's obviously more history here than I'm aware of."

"That's a true statement." He seemed indifferent to his surroundings and to the visit. "I feel like nobody can touch me now."

"Do you want out?" Toddrick asked sarcastically. "That's why we're here. To save you."

Jimmy raised his eyebrows. "I guess so. What I really need is for you to check on Norma. I think she might be in trouble."

"Who's Norma?" Lisa wrote the name down. "What's her last name?"

"Blackwell." He looked at Toddrick. "Remember? The reporter I had with me at the trial. The one writing everything down. She went with me to do some of the speed trapping on the police. I wanted someone credible to document what I was seeing."

"Which was what?" Lisa asked, getting to the heart of the matter, pen-poised to record his answer. "What were you seeing?"

"Nothing, really. Just cops speeding. But the last couple of days, I felt like someone was watching me." He pointed to his face. "Then this happened, and then Strein died. And suddenly things don't seem like just a coincidence." Jimmy slapped his hand against the gray cinderblock walls. "Which is why I don't mind being in here. Something's up. I don't know what, but you guys can figure it out, right?

Lisa wrote a few things down on her notepad. "What about the night Strein was killed? Do you have an alibi?"

"I was sleeping in my bed." Lisa stared at him, looking unsatisfied, and he continued. "Sadly, I was alone." Jimmy tapped his chest, about where his heart would be. "Toddrick and I went to bed around the same time."

"No one can confirm your exact whereabouts?"

"No, no one can vouch for me."

Lisa tapped the pen against her mouth. "And the hammer?"

"It's mine. Well, not really mine as much as it belongs to the family. I used it last week to pound some nails into a few tires. When I was done with it, I left it on the porch. I forgot about it."

"A few tires?" Toddrick looked confused.

Jimmy smiled. "Yep. Hammering nails into tires."

"Let me guess," Lisa interjected. "Strein's?"

He laughed. "Yep. Doesn't look good, huh?" His laughter continued. "I'm trying to be honest. Strein was a jerk and as crooked a cop as there ever was." Both Toddrick and Lisa stared at Jimmy, open-mouthed. Jimmy must have sensed their waning confidence. "Come on, guys. You don't think I killed him, do you?"

"You were kissing his girlfriend?" Lisa sounded mortified. "Fighting with him in public and pounding nails into his tires in your spare time?"

"I had to intervene. He was hitting her, he took money from her, and he crashed at her house all the time. I'll never understand why women go for guys like him. Melissa is way too hot for Strein. And his buddies were always over there too. She complained about them hanging around all the time."

"You intervened by trying to take his girlfriend?" She looked stunned.

Jimmy rolled his eyes. "I wasn't trying to take her from

anybody. I don't think she's a one-man kind of gal." Jimmy winked. "If you know what I mean. Still didn't kill Strein."

Toddrick crinkled his forehead and shot a glance at Lisa. "Not a one-man kind of gal," he questioned.

Lisa sighed. She shot Jimmy a perplexed look. "We have a lot against us."

"At least we have a place to start." Toddrick stood up. "We even have two places to start. There's Norma Blackwell. Then there's Melissa, Strein's girlfriend. I wonder why I haven't read about her in the paper at all." He turned to Jimmy. "What's her last name?"

"Halway," Jimmy answered. "Melissa Halway."

They stood up to leave, and Jimmy motioned for them to stop. "Guys, just a thought before you go." His smile faded, and his expression became serious. "Follow me on this one. I didn't kill Strein, which means there's a killer out there. I don't know what's happening, but something's wrong."

CHAPTER TWENTY-ONE

Jimmy had enlisted Norma Blackwell as a second witness to boost his claims' credibility. Norma was a young, aspiring journalist who worked for *The Daily Southern*, the local newspaper. It was a smart move to partner with someone who could make public Jimmy's observations.

Toddrick and Lisa approached the front door of Norma's apartment. For a split second, their swinging hands collided. Had it happened to two friends, to unconnected companions or ordinary people on an ordinary outing, it would have been an insignificant occurrence—something to be ignored. But Toddrick and Lisa had a deep history. There was a slight pause in their walk. The moment lasted half a second, but it was enough to put a long-forgotten feeling in the air. Both of them pressed onward, not willing to talk about whatever it was they felt when their hands touched.

Toddrick knocked on the front door, and it creaked inward. Already open. Darkness filled the empty doorway. A ferocious stench spilled out the door, forcing both of them to cover their nose and mouth.

"Ugh," Lisa said, her voice muddled by her hand. "What's that smell?"

"Stay behind me." Toddrick shoved the door open, and it bounced off the inside wall. He found the light switch and flipped it upward.

An incandescent light cast its glow throughout the room, revealing a disaster. Everything that wasn't broken was turned over or looked drastically out of place. Papers, books, furniture, and broken glass were scattered all over.

They tiptoed through the tiny living room, careful not to disturb the mess. "Norma," Toddrick yelled. "Are you here?" A faint buzzing sound filled the air. The sound was strongest in the direction of an open hallway that looked like the entrance into a small kitchenette.

A bare foot stuck out from under a thin kitchen table. The skin was white and blue, void of natural color. They stepped into the kitchen and took in the full view. A young woman with black hair lay face up on the linoleum, resting in a shallow but wide pool of dark crimson liquid. Her mouth was open, her eyes wide, like shock was last emotion she felt before she died.

Norma was dead. And by the looks and smell of it, she'd been dead for a while.

Lisa gasped, lifting her hand from her mouth to the top of her head. Toddrick pulled her away from the corpse.

"Can you call the police?" he asked.

She quickly nodded and closed her eyes. She started digging through her hand bag for her phone.

"Jimmy and Norma must have been on to something. This can't be a coincidence, can it?"

Lisa shook her head. "I don't believe in coincidences. But why kill Norma?" Tears ran down Lisa's face. "Why would someone do this?"

Toddrick surveyed the messy the apartment. "Whoever it was, they were looking for something."

Lisa stepped outside and made two phone calls. The first was a 911 call to report the dead body. The second was to Tad Shackely. In minutes, both the police and Shackely crowded the entry way to Norma's tiny apartment. The deputies tended to the crime scene, and Shackely tended to his frazzled fiancé.

Toddrick sat watching, looking displaced. A man spotted him and walked through the debris of the room to where he was seated on the ground. "You're Jimmy's brother?" He extended his hand, and Toddrick shook it. "I'm Detective Reed."

"Toddrick," he introduced himself. "And yes, he's my brother. Jimmy was the one who sent us here to talk with Norma."

The detective nodded. "Right. Jimmy led you to Norma. Norma, who is dead." He spoke like he was accusing Jimmy of wrong doing.

Detective Reed wasn't dressed like the normal deputies. He was in business casual clothes and wore his gun and law enforcement badge on his belt. "You don't see the problem?" Reed asked, his tone drenched in condescension.

"Other than two people are dead and my innocent brother's in jail?" Toddrick shook his head. "That seems like a pretty big problem to me."

"Well," Reed said, "what would you say if this girl Norma and Jonathan Strein were killed on the same night, and by the same person?"

"What do you mean?" Toddrick's voice was calm, but I recognized the tightness around his eyes and mouth. He already knew what Detective Reed was insinuating.

"I mean," the detective began, "your brother sent you here because he knew Norma was dead, because he killed her. Killers do that. They like to show off, help people solve their own crimes. Lead others to their victims." Reed snorted. "Your brother can't help but show off."

CHAPTER TWENTY-TWO

The hammer that smashed into Strein belonged to Jimmy. The knife they pulled from Norma's back also belonged to Jimmy. It was public knowledge that Jimmy and Strein had their disputes and that the day of his death, Strein and Jimmy fought. Jimmy's connection to Norma was less known, but after a thorough investigation of Norma's apartment, there was evidence that he'd been there. The evidence wasn't substantial or criminal in nature, but it connected Jimmy to the location. In addition to this, several officers saw Norma and Jimmy communicate through hand signals at court the day of her murder. Their connection was undeniable.

The most compelling evidence of all was the discovery of Jimmy's speed gun in the trunk of Norma's car. It had been stowed there along with a laptop that proved, after the police could get into it, that Norma and Jimmy had spent a significant amount of time together.

Jimmy faced two murder charges. Jonathon Stein and Norma Blackwell.

"Norma is dead?" Jimmy looked as shocked as he sounded. "They think I did it?" He shook his head. "You've got to be kidding me." He put his head in his hands. "Norma? I shouldn't have brought her into this. Whatever this is."

One of Jimmy's hands was wrapped in bandages that reminded me of a mummy. There was visible bruising of the exposed fingers.

"What happened to your hand?" Toddrick asked. "That looks painful."

Jimmy smirked. "I guess I'm not as safe in here as I thought."

Toddrick winced. "Inmates are rough, huh?"

"Not even close." Jimmy scoffed. "This was compliments of a few deputies. They came into my cell yesterday morning, almost immediately after you left. Started asking me about my phone. They wanted to know where it was." He held his hand up again. "I didn't tell them, so they did this. Said they'd be back again if they didn't find it. I guess they don't want me posting videos of them speeding."

"But you know where your phone is, right?" Toddrick asked. "It only has videos of them speeding?"

Jimmy shrugged his shoulders. "I think so."

"I hate to make things worse . . ." Lisa interrupted. "Tad doesn't want me working on the case anymore." She looked down. "He thinks you're guilty." Lisa swallowed and closed her notebook. "He suggests you get a lawyer."

There was an uncomfortable silence in the air. Jimmy looked at Lisa, his smile gone, his eyes intense. "Do you think I did it?" He held up his hand wrapped in bandages. "You think this is normal, deputies beating and threatening inmates? Okay, I'm sure it happens all the time, but theres something wrong with this stupid town."

Lisa leaned forward on the metal seat but kept her eyes on her knees. "The evidence is overwhelming." Her eyes finally lifted to meet Jimmy's. "Law Enforcement doesn't like it when one of their own is killed. They think you're a cop killer. If broken fingers is all that happens to you, you'll be lucky."

"Thank you for your help, Lisa." Toddrick touched her shoulder.

She looked at him, stress and sadness in her eyes. The grieving look on her face was no less than that on Toddrick's.

"It was really good to see you again." His eyes glistened in the frail jail light, but his tone was firm and dismissive. In his own way, he was telling her she needed to leave.

The color drained from her face, her normally tan skin transforming in seconds to a winter's coat. She opened her mouth, probably to apologize, but Toddrick didn't let her. "We appreciate all you did. Tell Tad thanks, too." Toddrick's face twitched, his muscles working extra hard, fighting the betrayal of his true emotion. "Don't wait for me. I'll walk home."

Jimmy looked on with wide eyes, aware of the unspoken tension between former lovers. Lisa looked at him through the plastic glass and then back at Toddrick. The uncomfortable silence didn't end. She stood up but didn't move. Her mannerisms and posture indicated she didn't want to go. She was waiting for an invitation to stay. When it didn't come, she left.

Jimmy's eyes welled with tears. "Thank you for not

abandoning me. I know you still love her." He gathered his emotions, blinking hard until he gained control. "I wouldn't blame you for going with her. Someone's setting me up. Why is this happening? Norma was a sweet girl."

"It's gonna be all right," Toddrick said. "You were right. You and Norma were onto something. I'm going to talk to Strein's girlfriend." He winked at Jimmy. "Hopefully she's not dead."

"That's not funny," Jimmy said. "Do you remember Melissa?

"Um, we've been talking about her, right?" Toddrick chuckled. "She's the reason you're here. Pssh. Kissing another man's girl."

Jimmy smiled. "When you see her, you'll remember her. Tell her I said hello."

"Um, okay." Toddrick shrugged. "Seriously, though, what did you do to cause this much trouble? It can't be about cops breaking the speed limit. Where are the videos you took of them speeding?"

Jimmy laughed. "On my phone, dummy."

CHAPTER TWENTY-THREE

The door jetted open two inches. Part of a woman's face appeared.

"Melissa?" Toddrick asked.

Her eyes scanned his face, and then she looked behind and around him. Toddrick was alone. "Yes," she said.

"I think you knew my brother, Jimmy." Toddrick put his hands in his pockets and rocked back and forth on his heels.

"Knew? He isn't dead, is he?" Mild concern washed across her face.

"No," Toddrick said. "He's in jail. Can I talk to you for a few minutes? Jimmy said he left his phone here. I was hoping I could get it."

Her expression changed to suspicious. She chewed on her lower lip, thinking. "All right," she said. The door closed, followed by the sounds of metal sliding as she unlocked the door. "Come on in. I didn't think you were going to make it."

"Make it?" Toddrick asked.

"Yes," she said, giving him no further explanation.

The house was well-lit and smelled like it had just been cleaned. It was an older house, but well-maintained. Toddrick sat on a couch across from Melissa, who crossed her legs and rested her arms in a rocking chair.

Toddrick examined her face. "Do I know you? You look familiar?"

"I see a lot of people," she replied. "Have you been here before?" Toddrick shook his head. "Well," Melissa said, "maybe before the night is over you'll remember me."

Something about the way she spoke put Toddrick on edge. Like maybe she knew something he didn't. He cleared his throat. "Jimmy said he was here a few nights ago and left his phone. Can I have it?" He shifted his body weight in the chair.

Now, I'm telling their story. The story of those two boys. But when you're dead and gone like I am, you look at things a little differently. When I was alive, it was hard to tell the good from the bad. Now it was like I saw a whole new side of people.

I'm telling you this because I could see the kind of person Melissa was. She wasn't good, and it wasn't because she was a hooker. Something about Melissa wasn't right. Something deeper than prostitution, lying, or cheating.

As I watched Toddrick move around in his chair, uncomfortable for reasons he himself couldn't identify, I feared for him. Melissa was as pretty as a summer's day, but inside that beautiful body was a rotting corpse.

Melissa gave Toddrick a beautiful grin, flashing white teeth. "Jimmy was here," she confirmed. She blew air out her mouth and fanned her cheeks. "Free of charge.

Jimmy is definitely exciting."

Toddrick shifted his weight again, looking more uncomfortable than before.

Melissa crossed her hands over one knee and leaned toward him. "Oh, don't worry, sweetie. I knew what Jimmy was up to, trying to get to Jonathan by kissing me." She laughed. "Making Johnny jealous isn't hard." Her eyes turned downward, the smile dropping from her face. "I liked the dual attention."

When she didn't say anything more, Toddrick asked, "Do you think Jimmy killed Strein?"

Melissa looked Toddrick up and down. Her shoulders relaxed and she leaned forward again, revealing cleavage.

Her eyes focused on some imaginary place. "It's all gonna come down anyways." She breathed heavily. "I'm not sure why people had to die. Nobody was supposed to." Her rocking chair creaked as she moved back and forth.

"No," she said. "Jimmy didn't kill Jonathan. Jimmy's too gentle. His heart is too kind."

Toddrick nodded in agreement. "Jimmy is good. Nobody knows it but me. I know Jimmy on the inside."

"I didn't say he was good," she corrected. She cocked her head to one side, and the edges of her mouth looked like they were going to rise into a smile, but they didn't. "But he isn't a killer. Strein was a killer."

Toddrick blinked. "What do you mean? Strein was a killer?"

She shook her head from side to side. "I don't know why people do the things they do." She sucked in a big breath of air, like a smoker would inhale a drag from a cigarette, except she didn't have one. "Do you know what pillow talk is?"

Toddrick raised his eyebrows. "I think so. Don't have much experience with it. Well, none really."

"Innocent," she snorted. "Or stupid. When you're the bed-mate of someone for a long time, you hear stuff. You go to bed together, wake up together, you find out about their day... what goes on in their life. Personal stuff. Boring stuff. Intimate stuff. Sometimes bad stuff."

Melissa had a faraway look in her eyes. She was sitting on her rocking chair, but her mind was somewhere else. She swallowed and broke her trance. "Something's been wrong with Jonathan for a long time."

"Have the police been to see you?" Toddrick must have wondered if she was another suspect in this murder. After all, wouldn't Melissa be the first place to start an investigation, having been with Strein day in and day out? "Did they have questions about Jonathan for you?"

Melissa smirked. "The police wouldn't come talking about that with me."

Toddrick looked confused. "Why not? You're the closest person to the victim."

"I said the police wouldn't come here to talk to me about Jonathan. They might come to talk about other things."

"Like what?"

A tear birthed from the corner of her eye. She wiped it away. "Pillow talk." Melissa stood and motioned for Toddrick to do the same. "You should go."

Toddrick didn't move. "Pillow talk? What does that have to do with my brother?" He sat motionless on the couch, watching her, his eyes wide.

She leaned close enough to kiss him and stopped. "Do you remember me?"

Jimmy had asked Toddrick the same question. He pressed his eyebrows together. "I'm trying to. Have we met?"

She sat back down in the rocking chair. "I was a junior in college. That's as far as I made it in school. I stayed up late with people I thought were friends. Got smashed. Drunk as drunk could be. Something I did a lot back then." She rocked back and forth in her chair. "It wasn't that long ago. Seven years, maybe. Probably the worst night of my life." Her voice was back in that faraway place. "I won't tell you the worst of what happened, but I hated every minute. Terrible, terrible things. Things that scarred my soul. I awoke the next morning, cold, half naked and abandoned under a tree."

Melissa looked at Toddrick and forced a smile. "Remember me now?"

Toddrick's face ignited with recognition. "Yes. Yes I do."

More tears fell from her eyes. "Two boys stopped on their way to football practice and took me out of the cold, bought me a coffee and took me home." She smiled. "Two sweet boys. Had it not been for those two sweet boys . . ." Melissa's voice trailed off.

Toddrick looked overwhelmed with the revelation. He was going to say something, but Melissa didn't let him.

"You need to leave," she directed. "Go. Get out of here. It's not safe for you." She pulled him from the couch and pushed back to the entrance of the house. At the front door, she removed a bundle of fake flowers from a long and wide vase. She reached her hand in and pulled out an iphone. It was a peculiar place to store a phone. It was almost like she was hiding it.

"Here," she said. "This is Jimmy's phone."

Toddrick took the phone and asked, "In the vase?"

"I have my reasons." Melissa looked out the tiny sliver of window by the front door. "Others have been here asking for it, but I saw reasons to hide it. Jimmy didn't kill Jonathan *or* Norma. It's all gonna come to an end soon. Watch Spook Lake for a few days. That's where the answers are. That's where I sent your lady friend."

Toddrick cocked an eyebrow. "Lady friend?"

"She's the one who told me to expect you. Said her name was Lisa?"

CHAPTER TWENTY-FOUR

Toddrick slid his finger across the screen of Jimmy's phone. It unlocked without a password. The battery was nearly dead, so he took it to his room and began to recharge it. He pressed the photos tab and flipped through the pictures. He had no idea what he was looking for, but maybe there was something that could help prove Jimmy's innocence.

The first few photos were of people: Norma, Melissa, and others Toddrick didn't know. There were photos of random places, and snapshots of the inside of Jimmy's bedroom. The photos shifted from shots of people to green patches of trees surrounding sections of gray water. Toddrick recognized the area. Spook Lake.

Amid the string of photos were several video clips. He pressed the little black triangle, and a video began to play. Jimmy's recorded voice streamed out the tiny speaker on the phone. "I've been here with Norma for almost fifteen minutes. I've taken her to one of the places where I catch a lot of deputy traffic."

The screen showed Norma's face. She waved and

smiled. "Hi."

"And," Jimmy's voice continued as the camera zoomed in on a radar gun in her hand. "We have a speed gun to capture speeding deputies." As if cued by a movie director, the faint rumbling of an engine grew in strength. "Check it out, check it out," Jimmy shouted to Norma. "Get the gun ready. Get behind that tree."

There was shuffling on the screen as Jimmy scrambled into position behind Norma, who had propped herself up behind a tree to shield herself from view. Headlights drew closer as a car sped down the country road. Within seconds, a deputy's cruiser swished past the camera.

"How fast was it going?" Jimmy asked excitedly.

"Yikes," Norma exclaimed. "Maybe that deputy was on his way to help someone."

"Yeah right," Jimmy spat. He zoomed the camera on the digital miles per hour reader on the back of the gun. The red neon lights displayed the two digits 8 and 9. Jimmy chuckled. "And there you have it, folks. Going eighty-nine in a fifty-five."

The clip ended, and Toddrick clicked the next black triangle on the screen. Nothing but trees and murky water. Toddrick didn't know where it was, but he guessed it was along the shore of Spook Lake. The image jumbled as Jimmy walked over uneven ground. The hoods of two police cruisers appeared on the screen, and then lights from another vehicle approached.

The video ended, showing nothing more. Just two police cars and a third car coming to meet them.

There had been lots of pictures of police cars. Toddrick couldn't tell if they were the same cars or not, but the civilian vehicles pictured were definitely the same. In almost every photo taken at the lake, Toddrick saw the same light blue truck.

That was it. No people, no shots of anything interesting, nothing out of the ordinary. Just a few patrol cars and civilian vehicles parked around Spook Lake. The police *should* be patrolling Spook Lake. It was a place that was known for dares, pranks, and general mischief. Other than catching some deputies speeding, the pictures were non-conclusive about anything that could get anyone in trouble. Toddrick set Jimmy's phone down, a disappointed look on his face.

Spook Lake.

That wasn't its real name. If you looked it up on a map, it would be called Treet Lake. Nearly a century ago, a woman and her daughter drowned in Treet Lake while swimming. Popular folklore said that at certain times of the night, you could see their ghosts swimming in the water or walking through the trees. You could walk through the area and feel the hair on your neck rise. It got a reputation of being a place for the damned. I can't remember when we started calling it Spook Lake, but the name stuck.

For the most part, people stayed away from the area. The water of the lake lowered with the seasons and attracted all kinds of insects. Occasionally, couples who were looking to be alone would try to find seclusion there, but even those were few.

Toddrick parked his car behind thick foliage blocking the main entrance to the Lake. The sun was setting, leaving a dim stream of light. He had less than one hour before it would be dark. From the trunk of his car, he grabbed a flashlight and covered himself with a black hoodie. He secured his phone in his pocket, stuck the flashlight in the front pouch of the hoodie, and walked toward the lake. He stayed hidden in the tall grass parallel to the dirt road.

He'd barely started walking when the sound of tires on gravel crept through the air. A vehicle was approaching. Toddrick ducked behind the bushes and waited for the car to pass. Around a bend in the road, pale lights lit the vegetation. A police cruiser slowly rolled up the gravel trail. It drove past where Toddrick was hiding, continued all the way to the edge of the lake, and nestled itself in a section of trees.

Toddrick walked in the areas that provided the best concealment. He crept toward the parked police car.

The sound of another vehicle approaching made him freeze. The second car seemed more cautious than the first. It was going slower and making less noise, taking its time. It was difficult to see against the darkening sky, but when it turned, it reflected the last light of the setting sun. Toddrick recognized it as the blue truck that Jimmy had captured on film.

The truck parked parallel to the patrol car, and their windows rolled down. Toddrick moved through the foliage quickly, trying to get a closer look at the drivers. His focus was on the two parked vehicles, so he didn't see the sedan hidden in the foliage, directly in his path. He nearly smashed into the back bumper, but at the last minute he saw it and diverted his momentum into a dive that placed him on the ground near the back of the car.

A woman sat in the driver's seat. She looked at the parked vehicles through a pair of binoculars. Slowly, Toddrick worked his way around the passenger side. When he saw her profile, his shoulders relaxed.

He tapped on the window.

Lisa put a hand over her mouth, and the binoculars fell to her lap. She reached over, unlocked the passenger door and waved him into the car. "You scared me." She put a hand to her chest.

"Sorry," Toddrick said, gently closing the car door. "What are you doing?"

She picked up the binoculars and put them back to her eyes. "Due diligence, I guess. I've been watching for a few hours. This is the second time deputy cars have been here today. Something's going on." She let the binoculars rest in her lap. "What are *you* doing here?"

"Trying to get Jimmy out of jail. I saw Melissa. She said I could get answers here." Toddrick bit his lip. "She said you'd been by to see her. Why are you doing this?"

Lisa's eyes dropped. "I'm sorry for what I said to Jimmy. I was wrong. I went to Melissa because she was the next lead. She sent me here, too." She looked at him, her eyes searching his. "I told her you would probably pay her a visit."

Toddrick met her eyes. "I understand why you question him. The evidence is pretty heavy. Besides, it's not like you owe us anything. You have your own priorities, and Jimmy and I aren't on the list."

His words hung in the air. He scooted forward in the seat to look at the two parked cars. "Why are we here? Can I borrow your binoculars?"

She handed them over, and he looked through the lenses. She smiled. "Because this is where it's happening."

"And that is what?" Toddrick asked, trying not to sound clueless.

"What I think Jimmy and Norma accidentally

recorded."

"Oh," Toddrick said. "I have Jimmy's phone. Melissa gave it to me." He pulled it from his pocket. "See?"

"Great," Lisa exclaimed. "Anything on it that helps? What's in the videos?"

"Nothing, really." He put the phone on the dashboard. "Just a few clips of cops speeding and cars parked like that." He pointed to the two cars by the lake. "Nothing out of the ordinary."

"Hmm." Lisa looked thoughtful. "Well, it's clear something is going on. Jimmy and Norma didn't know what they discovered. Something big is going on here." Lisa sounded excited.

Toddrick looked at her quizzically. "What do you know?"

"I know whose truck that is," she stated through a coy smile.

"Whose?"

"Judge Paxton's. I don't know why he's here, but I bet it's not good."

"That blue truck has been coming here for weeks," Toddrick said.

"How do you know that?" Lisa reached for the binoculars.

"Jimmy's phone has a bunch of pictures and videos of it."

"I so owe him an apology." Lisa squished her cheek to her face and wrinkled her nose. She lifted the binoculars back to her eyes.

"Hey." Toddrick pointed to her left hand. The day before, Lisa had been wearing a giant engagement ring, a symbol of her upcoming marriage to Tad. "Where's your ring?"

She put down the binoculars, her eyes welling with tears. "Oh, Toddrick," she cried. "I owe you an apology too." She looked at him, her eyes wet and searching. "I love you. I still love you. I always have."

CHAPTER TWENTY-FIVE

Now, I know I'm telling a story. I'm trying to keep the chronology straight and not litter you with commentary on this or that. I don't want to get sidetracked. But as a man who's fallen in love and still holds to that love, I think moments like this are important. Moments like when Lisa told Toddrick that she loved him. It was like the setting of things right.

As Toddrick and Lisa embraced that night, I couldn't help but feel a measure of satisfaction. I knew he loved her, and the thought that he would be forever separated from her was painful.

Matters of the heart should be simple. Either you love each other or you don't. If you do love each other, you should be together, right?

The reality of love is much more complicated. These days, finding a lasting partnership is rare. I have no crystal ball to see the future, but I figured Toddrick and Lisa were a couple that could be built to last. I was pleased that they'd come full circle. I couldn't have been happier for the two love birds, reunited and melting together in Lisa's car.

The joy I felt at Toddrick's renewed love was eclipsed by the despair I felt for Jimmy's predicament. Alone he sat in the county jail, accused of crimes he didn't commit. Imagine the duality of my emotions. Happiness on one hand, despair on the other.

Toddrick and Lisa traversed thc dark parts of the woods to keep from being seen. Coming from behind the parked vehicles, they had a clear view of the silhouettes getting in and out of Judge Paxton's pickup.

The sun had disappeared and the moon was low in the sky, but it provided enough light to reveal hands and arms making exchanges. The bed of the truck bounced up and down as two men threw dark bags off the tailgate. The bags looked like sandbags used to stop water in a flood.

The last of the bags hit the ground, and the men jumped out of the truck bed. One of them slapped the side of the truck with an open palm. "All right, Judge. See you later."

Paxton poked his head out the window. "Keep it down," he reprimanded. His voice became friendly, and he smiled. "That should be the last of it."

"It's about time." The man sounded condescending. "We don't want any more people to get in the way."

"Hush, now," the judge said. "One more, and we are done and out. We need to cool it for a bit. Take a break and lay low."

"That's what they all say," the man said. "Once you get a taste of the money, nobody ever slows down."

The two men grabbed a few of the bags at their feet and dragged them into the woods. Deep in the trees, one of them pulled a camouflaged tarp off a large wooden cart. It had a metal handle bar on one end, which made it looked like a modern version of one of those old pioneer handcarts. The men dropped their bags into the cart and returned to the pile for more.

By the time they finished loading the cart, it was brimming with brown bags. The police cruiser and the truck pulled away, and the men pushed the cart deeper into the woods.

Toddrick and Lisa waited until it was silent and all traces of movement had disappeared. Slowly, they ventured out of hiding and stood where the vehicles had been parked.

"What do you think that was about?" Toddrick asked. He looked in the direction the two men had taken the cart.

"I don't know. Should we follow them?" Lisa didn't sound like she wanted to.

Under normal circumstances, calling the police would be the right thing to do. However, these were not normal circumstances.

She walked to the forest where the two men had taken the cart. Her foot caught on something, and it tripped her.

"Are you all right?" Toddrick helped her to her feet.

"I'm fine," she said. "I tripped on something."

Toddrick bent down and examined the ground, where his searching hands found something. He lifted a large, dark sack. "Nice find, Lisa." He held it up for her to see. "Looks like they left a bag for us."

CHAPTER TWENTY-SIX

Toddrick emptied the contents of the burlap sack. A few tightly wrapped paper packages fell on the polished wood table.

"What do you think's inside?" Lisa asked.

"Drugs?" Toddrick guessed. "Not that I would know, but I've seen some movies. Insane! How could something like this be happening in Glenwood? And with Judge Paxton and the deputies."

He started unraveling one of the brown packages. Several translucent, plastic sacks half full of a white powder-like substance tumbled out. He shrugged his shoulders. "Yep, looks like drugs."

"Wow. Paxton and the cops are in on it." Lisa looked at Toddrick, her eyes wide and her hands open in exasperation. "How are we supposed to turn them in?"

"I can't imagine that the entire Glenwood Justice Department is in on it." Toddrick took a seat at the table and put one hand over his head. "It kind of makes sense now."

"What does?"

He looked at Lisa. "You were right. Jimmy had no idea what he'd stumbled onto. He thought he was recording deputies violating speed limits, but he was about to uncover this." Toddrick pointed to the bag of drugs.

"Do you think this is why Norma is dead?" Lisa asked. "Maybe they had a plan to kill Jimmy too."

Toddrick looked like he was considering that. "How does Strein fit into this?"

"He was probably in on it."

"Then why is he dead?"

"I don't know." She sat next to Toddrick and took his hand. "We should call Tad. He can help us." She reached for her purse. "I'll call him." She dug around for a moment and frowned. "Hmm. It's not here. Can you call me?"

Toddrick dialed her number and waited to hear the ring. He didn't, so she checked the car. A few minutes later, she came back inside the house.

"Darn it. It's not there either. Must have left it somewhere."

CHAPTER TWENTY-SEVEN

"The judge is smuggling drugs." Lisa dropped the sack of white powder on Tad's desk. She looked at him, the man who, a day earlier, had been her fiancé. "If Judge Paxton and his deputies are in on it, who do we go to for help?"

Tad fingered the bag of drugs. He didn't return Lisa's eye contact. Since she and Toddrick had arrived, he hadn't even acknowledged Toddrick, who was sitting in a chair at the far end of the office. "You said you both saw the exchange?" His eyes were still down.

"Yes," Lisa answered.

"And you say Jimmy is being framed. The reporter girl, Deputy Strein, and Jimmy are all collateral damage, people who were a risk of either discovering what was happening or blowing a cover." Tad still wasn't looking up from the desk. He spoke slowly and thoughtfully.

"Yes," Lisa confirmed. "Well, we don't know about Strein, but what can we do?"

Tad looked up, suddenly invigorated. "There's only one thing we can do. I'm going to start making some phone calls, get the Feds involved. They should handle this." Tad got up and started pulling binders from shelves and digging through papers. "In the meantime," he said to Lisa, still ignoring Toddrick, "collect all the evidence you can. The drugs are safe here, but if you can give me Jimmy's phone, the one with pictures on it, that would be good." He stopped gathering things. "Can you do that?"

She nodded.

"Great," he said. "Be careful. If what you say is true, there are some killers out there. This should be over as soon as I can involve the right people." He smiled for the first time. "Never tried to get a judge arrested before. I'm going to make some phone calls. We need to get on this fast." Tad paused, his eyes narrowing. "I love you, Lisa. And something tells me you're in danger for knowing what you know."

She blushed. "I'm so sorry, Tad. I didn't mean to put you through this."

Tad looked at Toddrick. "The week before you got home, Lisa said your name in her sleep. We'd talked about you before. Part of what makes me a good attorney is reading where things are going before they happen. When Lisa introduced you to me in the lobby, I was already preparing myself."

Lisa's mouth opened, obviously surprised at the revelation. Toddrick looked at her. She returned his gaze, and red spilled over her cheeks.

"Thanks, Tad . . . for understanding. And for helping with Jimmy."

"Get me that phone before I change my mind," Tad said. "Call me when you have it."

"I've got it here." Toddrick reached in his pocket and

pulled out Jimmy's phone.

"Great," Tad said as he slid the phone into a desk drawer. "Hang tight somewhere safe. I'll call you when a plan is in motion."

Outside Shockley's law office, there was a deputy's cruiser parked next to Lisa's car. As they approached, the window of the cruiser lowered, and a deputy smiled at them. "Hi," he said cheerfully.

"Hi." Toddrick took Lisa's hand and edged himself in front of her. "Can I help you?"

"I was doing my patrol last night at Spook Lake. Regular routine, you know. I saw a light or something flashing on the ground. Naturally, I was curious, so I picked it up." The deputy held up a cell phone with a purple plastic case. "Is this yours?" He looked at Lisa, the corners of his mouth edging upward in a crooked grin.

"No," Lisa said flatly.

The deputy lifted his eyebrows. "Oh. Really?" He slid his fingers across the screen and pressed a few buttons.

The cell phone in Toddrick's pocket began to ring. He didn't reach to take it out, and the deputy asked, "Aren't you going to answer it?"

"It's my phone," Lisa admitted. "Can I have it back?" She extended her hand, palm up.

The deputy stopped smiling. "I don't think so." He tossed the phone on the empty passenger seat. "Just you remember. We are investigating a murder. We have one suspect in jail. But maybe there are accomplices out there." Slowly, he pulled away in his cruiser. "Have a nice day, now."

"Great," Lisa exclaimed. "I've ruined us."

"It's going to be fine," Toddrick said. "Tad will get

people to help and this will get sorted out. We can wait at Jimmy's place."

Lisa pulled the car onto Toddrick's street and gasped. "What is he doing here?"

The concern in her voice was unmistakable. A blue truck was parked in the driveway, and Judge Robert Paxton sat on the front porch.

Lisa pulled the car to a stop. "Stay here," Toddrick said. He exited the car and Lisa stepped to his side, ignoring his admonition to stay behind.

Paxton waved. "Hello." His smile was broad and confident. "Come inside and let's talk."

"We're not going anywhere with you," Toddrick asserted, stepping between Lisa and the judge.

Paxton kept his smile, obviously seasoned at dealing with noncompliance. "I don't want anyone to get hurt. Let's see." Paxton put a finger to his lip. "Jimmy is in jail on murder charges, and your mother will be home later this afternoon. I could have a deputy stop by to tell her about a jail fight that ended poorly for your brother."

Behind Toddrick, two deputy cruisers pulled onto the street and parked next to Lisa's car.

"I just want to go inside and talk this out, privately, before something bad happens." Paxton opened his arms like he was inviting them in for a hug.

Two deputies joined Paxton. One gave Lisa's phone to Paxton. "I followed them from Shockley's. They might have told him. He's being followed."

The judge clicked his tongue, and his confidence momentarily faltered. "That's a shame. I like Tad. I'd hate for something to happen to him." The judge held up Lisa's phone. "Now, can we go inside and talk about this?"

Toddrick shook his head. "I'm not talking to you."

"Well, that makes this a little easier." Paxton nodded at the deputies. "Place these two under arrest." The deputies pulled their handcuffs and stepped forward.

"Arrest us for what?" Toddrick yelled. Before he could react, his hands were cuffed behind his back. Lisa yelped as a deputy cuffed her.

Paxton looked smug. "We've been watching Spook Lake for quite a while. Got some tips that there may be some drug trafficking going on. Last night a deputy found this," he lifted Lisa's phone, "near one of the known trading places.

"And," Paxton continued. "I think your little brother was in on it. Maybe Strein and Norma stumbled onto your extracurricular activities, so little Jimmy had to cover some tracks. That makes you an accomplice to murder." He smiled. "The devil's in the details, kids." He walked toward his truck. "We'll see if we can find out all the things you've been up to."

CHAPTER TWENTY-EIGHT

I never thought I'd see my children in jail, but those two were both behind bars. True, it was for crimes they didn't commit, but there they were. Lisa too.

Now I've already told you that I can't read minds or get inside people's feelings, but I know my two boys. Jimmy had been in jail for a few days already, and a few days here and there for his previous traffic violations. He was doing fine, comfortable, even. Toddrick, on the other hand, looked like he'd suffered a tremendous psychological defeat.

Maybe it was the fact that he'd returned home from his studies expecting something different than what he'd got. Or maybe it was because he'd been betrayed by the law, which before he'd held in such high respect, or maybe it was because he could do nothing while he was in jail. He couldn't bring the truth to light.

I'm guessing what bothered Toddrick the most was that the love of his life was somewhere else in the jail and he couldn't be sure she was safe. He could do nothing except trust a man on the outside to help. Trust a man who was once Lisa's fiancé. Tad had been told about the drugs and those involved. He'd said he was going to contact the FBI, but would he be effective? Was he working fast enough, and was he himself safe? Paxton said Tad was a target.

There were too many variables. Too many uncertainties. I'd seen Toddrick discouraged before, but when he entered the jail with his mattress rolled under his arm, his head hung lower than I'd ever seen.

"Toddrick!"

Someone called his name. His head lifted, and his eyes searched dozens of men dressed in black and white stripes. Across the room of black and white clothed men, a figure moved in his direction. It took a few seconds for him to make out the features of the approaching person, but there was only one person who would know Toddrick.

"Jimmy!" Toddrick's countenance lifted.

Jimmy embraced his brother. He turned to the other inmates in the cell block. "Look, guys!" Everyone looked at Jimmy, who had one arm around Toddrick. "I'm not the only criminal in the family!"

His friends cheered and shouted out greetings. From the looks of it, Jimmy had many friends in jail.

"What'd you do, bro? Kill somebody?" Jimmy winked.

Toddrick smirked. "That's not funny. You know I didn't do anything."

"Then we're in for the same thing." Jimmy took Toddrick's mattress and walked toward the cells. "It's okay. It's not as bad as you think in here. You get plenty of sleep, three square meals, and a bunch of new friends. And there are no ladies. Jail will give your heart time to heal." He patted Toddrick's chest jokingly.

"Lisa and Tad aren't engaged anymore." Toddrick smiled.

"What?" Jimmy punched Toddrick's arm. "I told you kissing another man's girl isn't all bad."

Toddrick rolled his eyes. "She's in here, too." Jimmy looked surprised. "A lot's happened in the last couple days." He threw his stuff on a metal bunk bed.

Jimmy listened to Toddrick's account of visiting Melissa, Lisa and Tad's breakup, and the judge's involvement in shuffling drugs.

"You were the one who led to the discovery," Toddrick said. "You thought you'd filmed them speeding or just parked by the lake. Nope. That's where they exchange the drugs. Paxton knew we stumbled onto him, so he had us arrested." Toddrick wiped his forehead. "Lisa and I are accomplices to the murder of Strein and Norma. Apparently we helped you kill them."

"Whoa." Jimmy soaked in the information.

"Yeah," Toddrick said. "We told Tad. He was going to contact the FBI. That was a couple hours ago." He shrugged his shoulders. "What can we do? Just wait for Tad to rescue us, I guess."

The auditorium speaker cracked, a sign that an announcement was about to be made over the speakers. "Inmates three-nineteen and two-seventy-four, you have visitation." The microphone made white noise and then clicked off.

"Nice," Jimmy said. "I've got a visitor."

"How do you know what number you are?" Toddrick looked confused. "Who would want to see you besides me?"

"The number's on your bracelet." Jimmy furrowed his brow. "Mom comes every day. I saw her this morning."

Jimmy closed his mouth and looked to the ceiling. "Hang on. We never get visitation in the afternoon. It's always in the morning."

"Hey, I'm number . . ." Toddrick read the digits on his band, "two-seven-four. Maybe Tad was able to get to the FBI after all, and they're here to get us out."

Toddrick and Jimmy were escorted to the visitation area by a large female deputy. She sat them down in front of the clear, thick plastic screen that divided them from their visitor.

Jimmy smiled wide. "Melissa! What are you doing here?" He looked her up and down. "Wow! You are dressed to kill. You look great."

She smiled. "Jimmy, you always make me smile. I'm going to miss you."

"Miss me? Where are you going?"

"I've got one more job to do, and then I'm heading out of here." She looked at Toddrick. "It's nice to see you again."

"Can you help us?" Toddrick asked. "I know who's responsible for killing Strein and Norma. It's Judge Paxton. He's got this whole drug operation, and half the sheriff's deputies are in on it. Tad Shockley knows about it. He should have contacted the FBI by now. Can you call him for us?"

Melissa shook her head. Her eyes were sympathetic. "Mr. Shackley got into a car accident a few hours ago. He's in the hospital in critical condition."

Toddrick's excitement withered. "What? Is he okay?"

"Great," Jimmy said, folding his arms. "We're stuck."

"No, you're not," she said. "You're not stuck. I'm going to get you out."

"Do you have explosives in your bosom?" Jimmy

asked. He eyed her chest.

She winked at him. "No, sweetie. But Tad *did* call the FBI. They're here, investigating what Tad told them. Paxton is clever, and his network is broader than you might think. He's quickly spinning the evidence into a story that blames the three of you for the murders and the drugs."

"The FBI just needs to talk to Tad." Toddrick was adamant.

"Like I said," Melissa repeated. "Paxton has a vast network, and Tad may not come out of the hospital alive."

Toddrick went white. "You mean someone is going to kill Tad while he's there?"

"Tad was supposed to die in the car accident, honey." Melissa's gaze was broken by something unseen, a thought thatbothered her. "I'm supposed to finish him off so the FBI never has a chance to hear from him."

Toddrick and Jimmy looked at each other. Understanding registered on their shocked faces. Melissa was part of Paxton's *vast* network.

"Why are you here?" Toddrick's tone was accusatory.

Jimmy's spoke softly. "Melissa, what are you going to do? You obviously know more than us. You know how to set this right, don't you?"

She met Jimmy's eyes. "Such nice boys." Her gaze lingered on Jimmy, and then drifted into a place that was neither here nor there. In her mind, she was far away again. Her eyes were fixed, honed in on something in the future. "Don't worry," she said, reengaging their faces. "You'll be safe." She got up and turned to leave. "Thank you for being kind to me."

CHAPTER TWENTY-NINE

According to the press, it was the Fed-Ex man who found Melissa dead. He was delivering a package to the address of Melissa Galway and, on his way to the front door, he noticed a faint but pungent odor. He thought nothing of it until he peeked through the door window and saw the dark silhouette of a woman hanging from a chandelier. The spooked but well-intentioned delivery man kicked in the door and confirmed what he thought he'd seen.

Melissa's body was already in a state of decay and according to the autopsy, she'd been hanging from the ceiling for almost two days before she was discovered. The blood had pooled into her legs and feet, causing them to swell and contuse. The weight stretched her neck thin, giving her a ghastly, unnatural look. In life she had been a beautiful woman. But the morose corpse, elongated, swollen and leaking, was a closer manifestation of her inner strife.

Taped to her chest was an envelope with a letter tucked inside. The letter, more actually a suicide note, took up three pages front and back. In her own words, she explained the emotional state of mind that had allowed her to slip into her current situation. A situation that, for her, could only be remedied by death.

Melissa had developed a dependency on crack cocaine during her college years. She'd been discovered as a user, arrested, and arraigned before Judge Paxton. He invited her to his chambers and, to her surprise, he made her a deal. Paxton had several opportunities to bring more money to the community. He had contacts, money, and he had drugs; all things Melissa wanted.

She consented to be one of Paxton's dealers, but as her note explained, "A deal with a bad man is an even worse deal." For special favors with Paxton and one deputy in particular, she received what she needed to live comfortably for nearly a decade.

Melissa's note listed half a dozen deputies involved in pushing drugs by handcart through the woods behind Spook Lake. A hidden trail ran three miles to a section of dirt road that connected to a frequented drug route. It was from there that crack was distributed to all the Southern states. Paxton was the mastermind of possibly the largest drug distribution hub in the country.

Paxton hadn't realized how close Jimmy was to uncovering his operation until the day Norma appeared in the court room with him. Once Jimmy claimed to have video of the Judge and the deputies consistently breaking the speed limit around Spook Lake, Paxton had to intervene on whatever Jimmy and Norma were documenting.

He couldn't risk exposure. He ordered Strein to kill Norma with Jimmy's knife and frame Jimmy for it.

Strein, however, had become uncontrollable. To

Paxton, Strein was a time bomb waiting to explode. Last in a long line of transactions great and small, Paxton tasked Melissa to kill Strein. In her letter, Melissa confessed to the murder. It was she who smashed his skull with Jimmy's hammer. Under the burden of guilt and no hope to escape from the demon she'd become, Melissa hung herself.

Those two and Lisa were set free.

CHAPTER THIRTY

There's a certain liminal space that exists in all our lives where we are in between. In between what, you ask? We don't really know until it's over. It's only after we are past the *in between* that we can look back and say, "I was between that and now I'm doing fine." The in between is different for everyone.

My between was a little longer than most, but not as long as some. I was so sure of myself when I left high school, confident that the world was mine to tackle. I entered college and thought I knew what I wanted to do, and for a time I thought I was doing it. But as I went through the motions of living the dream I thought I wanted, there was a certain unexplainable hollowness that followed me. I shouldered through my better judgment and kept on doing. Just doing. Doing and ignoring that hollowness.

I was headstrong, but my heart was weak.

That all changed when I met Summer. So my in between was from the day I left home to the day I married Summer. In my *in between*, I made mistake after mistake.

Somehow, most of us survive the in between.

Unfortunately, some of us never get out.

Jimmy had been in the *in between* stage of his life for a long time.

But, just like Summer pulled me out of my doldrums, someone pulled Jimmy out of his. Toddrick reached through the thick fog of life and grabbed his little brother, pulling him to higher ground.

After playing a key role in exposing Judge Paxton and his deputies, Jimmy lost his fire. He reveled in the victory but found himself with nothing left to do. He beat himself up over the death of Norma. He abandoned his efforts to record speeding cops and stayed in his room most of the time.

Toddrick reacted differently. Immediately after his release from jail, he found a job at the rice plant. Nothing glorious or fancy, but it would help pay for his last few semesters of college. .

Every day Toddrick came home and encouraged Jimmy to come to work.

Jimmy put up a good verbal fight with things like, "I need time to reflect on what I'm going to do," and "that job doesn't pay enough," and "those hours will mess up my sleeping patterns."

Toddrick took it a step further. Every day, Monday to Friday at four in the morning, Toddrick forced Jimmy out of bed. Jimmy complained, saying things like, "I don't feel good," to which Toddrick replied, "Who does at four in the morning?" He also tried, "I'm taking a vacation day," to which Toddrick replied, "You haven't worked long enough to earn vacation."

Eventually, Jimmy accepted the unhappy fact that if

Toddrick was going to work, so was he.

"How long are we going to do this?" Jimmy asked.

"Do what?" The car rattled as it drove down the bumpy dirt road.

Jimmy ran his hands over his face like he was trying to clean the sleep off. "Work, Toddrick. How long are we going to work?"

Toddrick chuckled. He maneuvered the car around a steep turn and punched the gas as the road straightened. "We might stop when fall semester starts. Couple months, maybe. It might be best to work through school, though. We can arrange our classes to fit our schedule. College is cool like that."

"Whoa, whoa." Jimmy sat up in his seat. "School? I'm not going to school, man."

"You need to. You're behind. Almost twenty-two years old, not a penny to your name, no education, and no direction."

Jimmy looked insulted. "Who are you talking to?" He looked around the car for other people. "I've got about a hundred grand left from Dad's money, and I'm living at home with Mom. I have no bills to pay, and I don't see that changing in the future. Just 'cause you spent all your money doesn't mean I did."

"Oh?" Toddrick lifted his eyebrows.

Jimmy looked annoyed. "Direction?" Maybe I don't have any, but who does? You?"

"I'm not saying I have direction, but education at college is way different than high school. It's so much better." Toddrick turned the car with the curving road. "It's fun."

"You and I have different definitions of fun," Jimmy said.

Vehemently opposed to more education or not, I could tell the conversation had an effect on Jimmy. Later that same day, it was Jimmy who started to talk about it.

"Besides," he said, catching Toddrick off-guard, "it's not like going to school is going to give me direction. It'll probably just confuse me. New ideas and all." He held his hands up and wiggled his fingers like he was casting a spell.

The next day, Jimmy brought it up again. "College is weird. The way I see it—it's kind of an oxymoron. Under the disguise of higher education, emancipated teenagers pretend like they're interested in learning more gibberish, and they end up wasting their time and money." He shuffled bags of rice on a conveyor belt. "You know Graig Bilow?"

"Yeah." Toddrick grabbed a bag of rice and launched it toward Jimmy. "I know him."

"Well, Bilow's gone to college, and he's supposed to be real smart. Half of what he says makes no sense. The guy has no common sense, and he can't get a job. As I figure it, you can go to college and come out worse than when you went in. Still stupid and with less money in your pocket." He stopped working and rested his hands on a rail. "See, if I go to college, I'll be forced to get a job."

"How's that?" Toddrick threw Jimmy another bag.

"Because I'll have spent all my money on school. I'll be forced to work because my money will be gone." He hefted a bag. "It seems like a step backwards. I'm pretty sure I'll end up just like Bilow, penniless, socially awkward, jobless . . . but educated. Supposedly."

Toddrick didn't raise his eyes from the mechanical belt. He repositioned a few bags. "Something tells me you won't be like that."

Jimmy ignored him. "And I don't know what I would study. I hate math, I hate science, I hate reading . . . if that's even a subject. What else is there?"

Toddrick winked. "You'll figure it out."

And he did.

One month later, Toddrick and Lisa looked at their school schedules online. They were sitting in the living room, maneuvering classes so they could spend the most amount of time together while on campus. It'd gotten them in a peppy mood.

Out of the corner of her eye, Lisa noticed Jimmy watching them. He was eating a bowl of cereal and shooting glances at them. "Jimmy," she asked, "aren't you going to school?"

"Oh," Jimmy said in mock dismay, "I missed the registration deadline and now it's too late." He shoved a bite in his mouth. "Maybe next semester."

"It's not too late," she said. "You can register as late as two weeks into the semester." She smiled. "You have plenty of time."

Jimmy furrowed his brow. "Oh."

"Come on, Jimmy, its college. You have to go."

Toddrick looked at Lisa. "Believe me." He flashed a sympathetic smile. "I've tried. If you can get him to go to school, you're a miracle worker."

She smiled, eager to take the challenge. "Jimmy, do you know how many girls there are at the university?"

Jimmy's ears perked at the prospect of girls, but he shook his head. "The last two girls I had lip suction with died. I'm gonna hold off on the ladies for a while. For their sakes."

Lisa rolled her eyes. "I'm not advocating you look for

lip suction. There are some great girls out there who could use a good guy." She drank from a water bottle. "You need your better half, and she could be wandering around on campus. Just waiting for you." She drank from her bottle again. "I can help you register."

"Hey," Jimmy exclaimed. "I thought you broke it off with Tad."

"I did."

His forehead crinkled and he pursed his lips. "Hmm. Then why are you wearing that engagement ring?"

She laughed. "If you don't know the answer to that, then you definitely need to wise up. It's back to school for you."

CHAPTER THIRTY-ONE

"**I** can't believe it." Jimmy threw a stack of papers on the table. "That was embarrassing."

"What was?" Toddrick and Lisa were sitting on the couch eating Chinese food. Several glossy, white cardboard boxes were scattered on the coffee table.

"Okay." Jimmy looked like he was about to confess a secret. "I tried to register for college this morning. Apparently you need a little more than money to get admitted."

Toddrick swallowed a mouthful of noodles. "Really. What more?"

"An ACT score higher than what I got." Jimmy slumped in a chair. "I let you convince me to go to school, and then my stupidity gets slammed in my face." He scratched at his chin. "I'll be working at the rice plant forever."

"Have some food. What'd you say your ACT score was?" The corners of Toddrick's mouth tightened in a suppressed smile.

"I don't want to talk about it." Jimmy looked at the food. "Orange chicken?" Lisa nodded and put some in her mouth. "I'm hungry." He examined the cartons.

Toddrick laughed, but he tried to disguise it by clearing his throat and coughing. He patted his chest.

"What?" Jimmy asked. "What's funny?"

Toddrick forced his expression to be calm, but the edges of his mouth moved up and down. "Really, what was your ACT score?"

"I'm going to beat you down." Jimmy jumped over the couch and tackled Toddrick. They were playing, but within seconds they were sweating and panting as they tried to counter each other's moves. After a few minutes of strenuous wrestling, they stood apart from each other, both resting their hands and knees.

"You're in pretty good shape, aren't you?" Toddrick stood up and rested his hands on his hips. "I've got an idea." He grabbed his jacket. "Come on." He pulled on Jimmy's arm. "There's more than one way into college."

The walls were lined with bleachers, but they were mostly empty. The gymnasium floor was full of men in sweat shirts and pants. They jogged in a large circle around the arena. The air was stale and smelled of old sweat.

"What's this?" Jimmy asked.

"Wrestling practice." Toddrick scanned the room and then pointed to a man with a clipboard. "Ah. Follow me." He jogged toward the man.

"Excuse me." Toddrick extended his hand in greeting, almost like he was a car salesman about to make a deal. "I'm Toddrick, and this is my brother Jimmy. He wants to try out for your wrestling team."

"Is that so?" the man said.

"I do?" Jimmy asked.

Toddrick pointed at him. "He's really good."

The man looked Jimmy up and down. "My roster is full. Sorry."

"What?" Jimmy crossed his arms over his chest, obviously offended by the way the man dismissed him. "I'll beat anyone on your roster." His voice rang with challenge. "Anyone on your roster," he repeated slowly as he pointed at the clipboard.

The man smiled and blew his whistle. "We'll see," he said. He turned around and yelled at the group of jogging men. "Circle up!"

The group of wrestlers formed a circle around the coach. They sat crossed-legged with their hands in their laps—a trained position. "Quick diversion today, guys. We have a young man who wants to wrestle on our squad." Coach turned and pointed at Jimmy. "Says he can beat any guy on our squad." He chuckled softly. "I'd like to see that." He motioned for Jimmy to come over and pointed at a man in the circle. "Petersen, stand up. Show him how we do things around here. And don't let me down."

The guy named Petersen took off his sweatshirt and bounced around like he was loosening his muscles. A blue singlet clung tightly to his body. The muscles on his arms and shoulders were well developed and defined. He was of average height, but his muscles looked nimble and tenuous. Jimmy stepped into the ring of men, removed his shirt, and tightened the belt around his pants.

"I obviously don't have a singlet." Jimmy glared at Toddrick. "Didn't know I was doing this." He looked at Petersen, who was still bouncing around. "Hope you don't mind wrestling a half-naked man."

Jimmy's exposed upper body boasted an array of well-defined abdominal muscles. Like Petersen, his arms were muscular.

"Two minutes, fellas." The coach blew the whistle, and the two circled each other. Petersen lunged for Jimmy's leg, but Jimmy flattened his body on top of him and spun around on his shoulders. Bursting with speed and power, he pushed Petersen hard against the mat. He struggled to get free, but Jimmy trapped his arms around Petersen's chest. Then he bent Petersen's arm toward the ceiling, creating an unnatural angle for Petersen's elbow and shoulder joints.

Petersen winced in pain and strained to get Jimmy off his back. After he'd locked Petersen's arms, Jimmy rolled him onto his back. He held him there for five seconds until the coach reluctantly blew the whistle.

Petersen punched the mat and sprang up quickly. He was eager to show that he had a lot of energy left in his tank. "Sorry, Coach. The kid surprised me." He retook his spot in the circle of men and sat down, his eyes lowered.

The coach looked thoughtfully at Jimmy and then at the circle of men. "Sweeney, get up here." A man stood up and removed his shirt and pants, revealing the same blue singlet and chiseled muscles. He took his position in the center of the ring. Jimmy took his position opposite Sweeney, panting, still winded from the match with Petersen.

"Two minutes," Coach said again. The whistle blew.

Jimmy and Sweeney lunged for each other at the same time. Their shoulders locked and their muscles tightened and contracted. Their movements mirrored each other. When one pulled, the other pushed and when one pushed, the other pulled. For two solid minutes, Sweeney and Jimmy moved and counter-moved, but made no headway with each other. They both were fast and strong. Neither could get the advantage over the other.

It was a very boring two minutes.

The coach blew the whistle and ended the contest. "Okay, everyone, get on with practice. You," he said, pointing to Jimmy, "let's talk." Jimmy nodded and stepped closer. "Tell me, son, have you wrestled before?"

Jimmy pointed to Toddrick. "Just with that dirt bag over there."

"Well, the guy you just spared with is Tom Sweeney. Heard of him?"

Jimmy shook his head. "Sorry." He leaned over, trying to catch his breath.

"Sweeney is a national placer in his weight division. He had a bid for the Olympic trials last year, but lost in the second round. If you can hold your own against him, you can hold your own against anybody." Coach held up the clipboard. "Can I put your name on the roster, then?"

Toddrick jumped next to the coach. "Yes. Sign him up." He threw Jimmy's shirt at him. "Put your shirt on, goof ball. Get ready to register for classes."

Coach lowered the clipboard and looked at Jimmy. "You aren't registered for classes? You are going to school here, aren't you?"

"About that," Toddrick said. "We need your help."

Coach looked suspicious. "What kind of help?"

Jimmy sighed. "My test scores were too low. I tried to register for school, but I was denied on account of my

ACT."

Coach eyed both of them and started to laugh. "Test scores be damned. I'll make a phone call after practice and you'll be good to go." His laughter died. "Look around, kid. We ain't the brainy bunch, but we're here."

CHAPTER THIRTY-TWO

That first semester of Jimmy's life was probably the happiest I'd ever seen him. Though he outwardly ascribed to the inconsistencies of organized education, he was eagerly engaged. Learning became a challenge for him, a type of quest.

Most surprising to me, and probably to Jimmy himself, was that he was good at it. College and learning, I mean. A change came over Jimmy as he read books and wrote thoughts down. He found that he was smart, that he could think, and that the world respected intelligence.

Not only did he erase the effects of a low ACT score, but in his classes he was a top contributor. His opinion, which he shared often, was always on point. He also proved to be a first-class wrestler. After winning his first couple matches against seasoned athletes, Coach Blackenship trusted in Jimmy's tenacity. His teammates enjoyed having him around, and that made Jimmy feel accepted. Bouncing between classes, homework, and wrestling practice took away most of his free time.

He was still Jimmy, non-compliant and aggressive. But he was happy.

The greatest contributor to his happiness came when he least expected it. He was wearing a baseball cap with his hair tucked underneath, and he had a pencil behind his ear. He was a few minutes late to his American History class, so he was walking at a fast pace to get there. As he rounded the corner of the campus bookstore, he collided with a petite young woman.

The impact knocked her to the ground. She screamed in surprise, her books and papers scattering in the air.

"I'm so sorry." He knelt by her side and grabbed a few loose papers. "Are you all right?"

She eyed him warily. "I think I'm okay." She patted her cheeks and forehead with her hands and then looked at them as if looking for signs of damage. "You startled me."

"I'll get your books." He started to gather them up and noticed she was still on the ground. He dropped the books and extended his hand. "Hang on, I'll help you up."

With a strong, smooth pull, she stood on her feet again. "Thanks," she said. "I probably should watch where I'm going."

He looked at her, his eyes scanning her face.

I wasn't in Jimmy's mind, but I saw his face in that moment. I knew something was happening inside his brain, some chemical reaction that no scientist will ever be able to explain. It reminded me of a hypnotized cartoon character, with their eyes spinning round and round or popping outward. She was a pretty girl, but Jimmy was looking at her like she was more than just pretty.

I recognized that look.

Once, when I was a boy, my dad took me hunting. While driving a dirt road, three deer galloped across our path. Dad quickly pulled the truck off the road and handed me the loaded rifle. "Here, son," he said. "Shoot the one with the antlers."

Of the three, there was only one with horns. So I took aim and fired.

I missed, but an explosion of rocks erupted at the buck's feet, evidently where my bullet had gone. The animal bounced a few feet away, then stopped and stared at me. I smiled at the second chance to shoot him. I aimed again, shot, and the bullet disappeared into thin air. The buck walked a few steps away and looked back at me again.

For the third time, I aimed the rifle and fired. My first two shots must have been good practice. The buck jumped in shock, and red liquid spilled down the side of his light brown fur. His walking slowed, and then the buck collapsed. When I got close to it, I could see his eyes watching me and his chest heaving in and out. I put another bullet behind its ear, expediting death and easing pain.

My young mind was untrained to the hunt, and I hadn't expected the animal to just stand there like a giant target as I took shots at it. "Dad," I said, "why didn't it run away?"

"Son," he said as he started to cut the buck's belly, "those other two deer this fella was traveling with were females." He looked at me with knowing eyes, like he had just answered my question. He must have seen that I didn't understand the significance. "They were does, and they were in heat."

"Heat?" I asked.

"Yep." Dad pointed in the direction of the two deer that'd disappeared over the hillside. "They were girls, and this guy wanted them. He wanted them so much that it made him lose track of life." Dad looked at me, a bloody knife in his hand. "Made him kind of crazy, like all he could think about was being with those deer."

"That makes no sense," I said.

"You may not understand it now, but you'll see it again." He continued to gut the buck, pulling his knife through internal organs. "But it probably won't be on a deer." He paused and looked at me. "This happens mostly to men and women. They lose track of life when they want something too much."

The way Jimmy looked at Melodee Hastings that first time, the way his eyes were both alive and hollow, the way he paused before he asked her name, the way he repeated it back to her when she'd said it, all reminded me of that dead buck.

Lost track of life.

I was scared for my son.

So many men dash their lives upon the rocks of life for a woman. I'd wager society's prisons are full of men who, in the heat of the moment, lose track of what's important. They forgot that on the other side of the hill are greener pastures.

I can't speak for women. To a man, woman is life. I've never been good at math, but I know one valuable equation: Loving a woman costs life. It demands your whole heart, all your soul. Woman equals life. Simple math. Simple man.

The chances of knocking a girl down and then sweeping her off her feet are pretty slim. But Jimmy has a strange way of making things work. He never made it to his American History class that day. But he did make sure Melodee got where she was going.

In the wake of their blossoming affection, everything else melted into the background. The two were almost inseparable. As a father, I watched in nervous anticipation. Love is wonderful, but like I said, something about it makes people crazy. We say lovesick for a reason.

Jimmy and Melodee lived the entire semester like they were on cloud nine. He was in love, and the world loved him back. For two full semesters of college, they were connected at the hip.

Yet, I could see the storm behind the clouds.

It was the close of winter semester. Jimmy and Melodee had taken time to prepare for final exams. In the evenings, they would get together for a few wanton kisses and lingering embraces. All lovers do. As they had study groups forming to help prepare for exams, they found themselves skipping a few of their habitual late night rendezvous.

One evening Melodee told Jimmy she'd be busy preparing for her physical science exam. She would be locked in a study group for most of the night. There were a few classes on campus with reputations for destroying grade point averages, and physical science was the most notorious. Jimmy was eager to help, but she declined, explaining that her study group would probably be distracted with a newcomer.

"I need to focus, baby," she told him.

Jimmy was headed off-campus when he got a call from Toddrick. He and Lisa were going bowling and wanted Jimmy and Melodee to come along. Melodee was engaged with her study group, but Jimmy wanted to pass the time, so he went.

Surprisingly, the bowling alley was packed. Semester's end had brought many people to the normally unpopular sport.

They were a few rounds into their first game when Jimmy stepped up to bowl. He walked to the alley and swung his ball backward, ready to throw it down the lane without aim or care. He did not consider bowling fun, but making fun of it was. But on this particular turn, something happened that would forever ruin him and bowling altogether. He was about to swing his arm forward when he stopped, and his jovial disposition disappeared.

He looked at Toddrick. "Did you hear that?"

The sound of pins toppling against hard wood cascaded throughout the alley. "Uh," Toddrick said, scrunching his forehead in concentration. "I hear a lot of things. Is this a good song?"

"No," Jimmy said flatly. "I heard something." The look on his face was hard to describe. It was both frantic and worried, like he was in the emergency room waiting to hear if someone he cared about was alive or dead. It was a look that didn't belong in a bowling alley. He looked around the room, still clutching the bowling ball in one hand. His eyes scanned groups of people, searching for something.

It was Lisa who saw her first. "Oh, Jimmy," she said. She stepped to his side and took his arm, holding him tight with both her hands. Jimmy and Toddrick followed her eyes.

A few lanes away, a group of students played and laughed out loud, releasing the pressures of a college semester completed. Nothing they were doing should have drawn attention to them, but for Jimmy, it was who he'd heard laughing that stopped his world.

Under normal circumstances, the sound would have brought joy to his heart like it had many times before. It was a light and airy laugh, a sound he loved to hear and worked to produce. He hadn't expected to hear it now, in a low-lit bowling alley. It was a laugh that should have been in a study group somewhere, preparing for a physical science exam.

Several lanes away, Melodee sat in a small group of people. She was engaged in conversation with a young man, laughing at something he'd said. The man sput his arm around her. Melodee didn't move away or avoid his touch. She looked comfortable under his arm.

Jimmy dropped the heavy black bowling ball. It made a loud cracking noise as it bounced off the bowling platform. The crashing sound was so irregular to the sound of pins toppling that people looked in Jimmy's direction. Immediately Melodee stood, her face a twisted expression of panic. She took a step in Jimmy's direction, but he held out his hand to stop her. She ignored him and walked across the lanes until she was a few feet in front of him.

"Jimmy," she said, "I'm sorry."

He cleared his throat. "Is that your study group?"

She looked at him, trying to gauge the hurt on his face. I'd seen him hurt many times, but I have to say that the sorrow that registered on his face broke all my resolve. In death I wept for him.

"I'm sorry," she repeated. "I didn't expect you to be here."

He moved his head back like he'd been slapped in the

face. His lips tightened, and the skin around his chin twitched like he was fighting back words. Words he wanted to shoot like a machine gun. Instead, he turned and walked toward the door.

He walked past the checkout desk, and the bowling attendant yelled, "Hey, don't forget to return your shoes."

Jimmy kept on walking, oblivious to everything and everyone around him.

CHAPTER THIRTY-THREE

'd like to say that Jimmy handled his heart break well. But that's not how it went. In the end, Melodee found love and married the man she'd left Jimmy for. She was out of Jimmy's life almost as fast as she'd come into it. It was a little ironic; he'd run into her with a bang, literally knocking her to the ground. And she left him with her own bang, emotionally knocking Jimmy to despair. The light that had begun to grow inside him dimmed, and with it, the excitement of education. Once again, Jimmy withdrew into himself.

True to form, Toddrick did all he could to keep Jimmy engaged in life. Everywhere he went, he dragged Jimmy with him. Jimmy didn't enroll in college the next semester, but Toddrick signed him up behind his back.

Toddrick rented an apartment a few blocks from campus. Jimmy refused to move in with him, but Toddrick wouldn't take no for an answer.

Jimmy spouted a long list of reasons why he needed to stay close to home. "Besides," he said. "I'm comfortable here, and I don't want to spend money on a new apartment."

"Come on, man." Toddrick picked a plastic bag full of clothes off the bedroom floor. "This is the last of my stuff. I'll put it in the car, then I'll come back and we'll start to pack yours."

Jimmy shook his head. "I'm not packing anything. Seriously, I'm staying."

"I need your help to pay the rent. A two-bedroom apartment is expensive."

"Lisa will move in with you. You guys are going to be married in a year, anyways." Jimmy lay back on his bed. "You can probably get some practice time living together."

Toddrick dropped the bag of clothes and cocked his head to one side. "You know I won't do that."

"It's what everyone does."

"Not everyone."

Jimmy rolled away from Toddrick and faced the wall. "Whatever. Just leave me alone."

Toddrick sighed. "Okay, at least come help me unpack. I've got a ton of stuff, and I could use an extra hand."

Jimmy sat up. "Great. If it will get you out of here, I'd be glad to help."

It took an hour to drive across town and unload Toddrick's possessions. Just as they were unloading the last box, Lisa and Summer pulled into the parking lot.

"Hey sweetie," Summer said as she kissed Jimmy on the cheek. Toddrick was moving the last box up the stairs to the apartment. "I got your text," she shouted at him. "We grabbed the stuff you forgot."

Lisa popped the trunk of the car. "Come on, Jimmy. Help me get this stuff upstairs."

Jimmy reached for a box in the trunk. He examined the contents and stopped walking. "Hey, this stuff is mine."

"Of course it is, honey," she said. "Who else's would it be?" She lifted a box and started walking up the stairs. "It's okay." She grunted under the load. "Toddrick told me you guys didn't have enough room to take it all in one trip. The neighbors are bringing your bed in a few minutes. They have a truck."

As if cued by a stage director, Jed Applewood pulled his truck into the parking lot. "Howdy," he said to Jimmy as he drove by. It took seconds for him to park the car and start moving the bed out of the truck.

"Hey, Jed." Toddrick grabbed one end of the mattress. "We'll take this one to Jimmy's room." He grunted as he lifted. "It's the second bedroom on the right."

Jimmy rested his hands on his hips. "Really, Toddrick. I hate you."

And so it was that Toddrick and Jimmy got an own apartment closer to campus. It was like a bird spreading its wings and taking flight. It was the symbolic removal of all safety nets.

More importantly for Jimmy, even though it was a change forced upon him, it offered a change of environment. And that change in environment meant greater opportunity for change.

As always, Toddrick was a consistent and buoyant life jacket, and he wouldn't allow Jimmy to sink. Jimmy's depressed emotional state lent itself to poor lifestyle choices, but Toddrick always appeared and pulled him out of serious trouble. Ever vigilant, Toddrick watched over his little brother, blocking many attempts by lesser ideals to drag him down. Jimmy didn't succumb to numbness because Toddrick always intervened.

As a father who couldn't be there for his son, I was thankful for the crutch that Toddrick proved to be. He had been Jimmy's savior many times in the past, but it was at this time in Jimmy's life when he needed it the most. Had it not been for Toddrick, something tells me that Jimmy never would've recovered.

Jimmy started going through the motions of life again. He still lacked some of his usual fire, but there was enough energy around him to artificially sustain him. Before long, acting became reality, and Jimmy rejoined society fully rehabilitated.

Things settle back to normal.

Warm summer nights led to late night games or movies at Lisa's apartment. She had already graduated from college and lived with a group of friends still working their way through their own educations. Toddrick and Lisa made sure Jimmy came over as often as possible. They were hopeful that one of Lisa's roommates would rekindle his heart.

"UNO!" Jessica shouted. She held the last card to her chest and grinned excitedly. Jessica was the prettiest of Lisa's roommates, but by far the least ambitious with her life. College for her was a parade show where she could put herself on display until she captured a provider. Tonight, she was trying to capture Jimmy's attention.

"Your turn, Lisa," Toddrick said. "Play something good. You can't let Jessica win."

"Let's see." She made a humming sound as she sifted through her cards. "What to play, what to play?"

Pounding on the ceiling shook the room.

"Wow. What was that?" Toddrick glanced at the

ceiling. "If that happens again, your ceiling's gonna collapse."

Jessica shook her head. "It's our stupid neighbor and her stupid boyfriend. They always argue. I think the landlord is evicting them." She rubbed her nose. "Nobody wants them here, anyways."

"I feel sorry for her," another roommate said. "Faye's sweet, but her man is a total douche."

"You are who you hang out with," Jessica retorted. "If her man is a loser," she shrugged her shoulders, "so is she."

Another large crash came from above. A male voice boomed obscenities. "Give me the phone," he bellowed.

"You're hurting me," a woman's voice cried. A high pitched scream sounded from above. "Stop it!"

"Someone call the police," Toddrick commanded.

Jimmy jumped up from the table. Before Lisa had even begun dialing for the police, he'd opened the front door and stepped onto the metallic grid that made the front porch. Toddrick was just behind him.

Lisa pressed three buttons on her cell phone and started talking to someone on the other end. From above, there was a sound of something heavy sliding across the floor, like a couch or a table, followed by the sound of breaking glass.

"Leave me alone," the woman shouted.

Vibrations shook the entryway as someone rapidly descended the metal stairs above them.

Two bare feet appeared at the top of the stairs, and then bare legs up to the thighs. The girl wore jean shorts under a small white T-shirt barely concealing her shapely chest. She cradled one of her hands against her collar bone and ran straight past Jimmy and Toddrick into Lisa's apartment. "He's drunk," she said, whimpering, "and high."

From somewhere above, a door slammed. Heavy and fast footsteps shook the metal stairwell. "Don't you run away from me!"

"Better get inside," Toddrick said to Jimmy. "I'll hold him off until the police get here."

"Right," Jimmy said sarcastically.

A man appeared at the top of the stairs. He was either naturally gifted with an incredible physique, or he'd spent a lot of time in the weight room building his body. He was tall and shirtless, his muscles thick and twitching. Concealing his muscles was a thick layer of fat, but it only made him look more intimidating.

Toddrick held his hand out, palm up, the universal signal for stop. "You can't come in here."

The man stopped on the metal landing. In one second, he sized up Toddrick and Jimmy. Apparently, he didn't think they were a threat. "Don't try and stop me." He saw the girl through the apartment window and stepped toward the open doorway.

He was halfway into his first step when Jimmy shot past Toddrick and tackled the man's legs. In one fluid motion, Jimmy hefted him up. It took a moment for the man to realize that he was no longer on solid ground, but by the time he did, it was too late. Jimmy had the man a full body's length in the air before he spun him horizontal and slammed him on the metal entryway.

Jimmy dusted off his hands. "That should end it."

"Jay's drunk and high," the girl shouted. "He won't feel pain. He's only gonna get mad."

Jay pushed off the ground and started throwing punches at Jimmy. He was strong, but whatever drugs were in his system slowed him down and threw off his aim. Jimmy easily avoided his blows.

Jimmy ducked a heavy handed swing and lifted Jay by the legs again and knocked him to the ground. Using a well-practiced wrestling move, he tied up Jay's arms and locked him in place. Jay struggled and yelled against the pressure of Jimmy's hold.

"He's strong," Jimmy grunted. His face was red with exertion. "Did someone call the police?"

"They're coming," Toddrick yelled. He circled Jimmy and Jay, wanting to help, but the angle made it difficult. The two fighting men didn't stay in one position long enough for Toddrick to know who was who. It looked like a rolling pile of body parts.

Jay finally broke free and landed a punch on Jimmy's chin. The impact sent Jimmy sprawling. Toddrick took the opportunity to engage Jay. Two heavy-handed right hooks smashed into Jay's face, but it had no effect on him. He was quick to return the punches.

As Toddrick dodged the devastating swings, Jimmy sprang back to life. He pushed Toddrick inside the apartment and closed the door on him. "I got it," he yelled.

Jay's eyes were glazed and his lips looked wet, like he'd just drunk something and only part of it got in his mouth.

Jimmy countered Jay's aggression with punches of his own, but his efforts had no effect. Employing another wrestling technique, Jimmy forced Jay to the ground. Wrapping his arms around Jay's neck, he secured him in a strong chokehold.

"Stop moving or I'll cut off your air," Jimmy yelled.

Jay responded by kicking and bucking. He extended

his legs and flung his bent knees toward Jimmy's face. Jimmy tried to position his head so he wouldn't get hit by the blunt missiles, but Jay's knee cap slammed into Jimmy's forehead. Jimmy, stunned by the blow, momentarily loosened his grip, but regained his position after he recovered.

From the look on Jimmy's face, the knee he'd just taken to his head made the fight more real. Jay's tolerance for pain was through the roof. He'd been punched multiple times, been slammed on a metal grate and choked, and still showed no sign of quitting.

Jimmy tightened his arms around Jay's neck and squeezed. Jay struggled for a moment, but Jimmy exerted himself, his muscles refusing to yield.

Toddrick was back on the porch again, eager to help Jimmy secure Jay. But Jimmy had finally put Jay out of commission. The struggle ended when Jay lost consciousness, his head toppling heavily onto Jimmy's arm.

CHAPTER THIRTY-FOUR

By the time the police took custody of Jay, he'd regained consciousness, and a more substantial struggle ensued. Jay broke free from the officers and smashed one's face with a wild elbow. Taser guns fired, sending Jay into convulsions on the asphalt parking lot. Only after he was handcuffed and anchored to the ground by the weight of several officers did a medic come and review his condition.

"He's pretty beat up," the medic said. He wiped blood off Jay's forehead. The cast iron entryway and stairs had cut Jay all over his body. The medic shined a light into his eyes. "His pupils are dilated. What's he on?" The medic looked at the group around him, expecting someone to know. When no one responded, he said, "I have to take him to the hospital. He can ride in the ambulance as long as a few officers come with me and he stays handcuffed."

"I'll ride with him too." Faye stepped forward. She kept her eyes on the ground, embarrassed. She walked past Jimmy and raised her eyes to look at him. "I'm sorry for that." She pointed to the large bump on Jimmy's forehead. Jay's knee had smashed Jimmy's head there, leaving a lump the size of a golf ball. "Thanks for helping me."

"No problem," he responded casually. "You look a little cold. Would you like my sweater?"

She shook her head, and the medic shone the light on Jimmy's forehead.

"Did that just happen?"

"Yeah." Jimmy nodded his head toward Jay. "He gave me a few lumps before he went down."

The medic got closer to Jimmy and examined his head. "It looks really bad. How does it feel?"

"Honestly? Not very good. After he hit me with his knee, I couldn't afford to get hit again. Not like that." He placed a hand on his head and winced. "That's why I choked him."

"You're lucky," the medic stated. "Whatever drugs he's on's been mixed with alcohol. Makes him stronger than an ox and repellent to pain. He could have killed you without knowing it." The medic ran his finger along his clipboard. He looked at Jimmy and then at the ambulance. "I recommend you get that checked out. It *really* doesn't look good. There's room for one more in there."

"No, thanks." Jimmy shook his head and then grimaced, like the movement was painful. "I'll sleep it off."

"I'll take him," Toddrick volunteered. He pulled his keys out of his pocket and jangled them. He winked at Jimmy. "You should have let me help." He put his arm around Jimmy. "Why'd you do that, anyways, take him on like that?"

Jimmy smiled. "She's super-hot," he whispered.

"Who?" Toddrick raised an eyebrow. He followed Jimmy's eyes to the ambulance. Faye was climbing into the open rear door. "Oh man. Give me a break. You really need to see a doctor."

While they sat in the ER waiting area, Faye walked through a pair of swinging doors. When she saw Toddrick and Jimmy, she quickly changed direction. She sat on the opposite side of the room and lifted her feet on the chair, tucking them underneath her.

Even though it was late summer time, the temperature had dropped with the night, and the air conditioning in the waiting room was working fantastically well. Faye looked cold in her short shorts, flip flops, and white tank top. Her skin had a tinge of blue to it, testifying of the blood vessels working overtime to heat her body.

Jimmy sat down next to her. She looked at him cautiously and leaned her body away from him.

"How is he?" Jimmy asked.

Faye had that uncertain, fearful look, like she wasn't sure what Jimmy was going to do to her. She looked like a balloon waiting to be popped. When it didn't happen, she let go of all the tension inside. "He's fine." Her defensiveness softened, and she exhaled.

"And how are you?"

Faye squinted at him, a little redness in her cheeks. Her chin began to quiver, and her eyes filled with tears. "I'm," she tried to hide her emotions, "fine."

"You'll be okay?" He took off his hooded sweatshirt and held it out to her. "You look freezing. Put this on."

She took the sweater and wiped her nose with it. She looked at the sweater, the mucous and tears she'd just put on it, and then at Jimmy. Realizing she'd used his offering as a napkin, she started to cry again. "I'm so sorry. I have no idea what I'm doing."

Jimmy laughed. "It's okay."

A young-looking nurse entered the overflow through the double doors and approached Jimmy. "Here's your prescription for swelling and pain. Be sure to ice your bump." She glanced at Faye and walked away.

Toddrick stood up. "You ready to go?" he said, looking at Jimmy.

"Yeah." Jimmy nodded at Fay. "You want a ride, or are you waiting for your boyfriend?"

"He isn't my boyfriend anymore." She put her head in her hands. "It was never supposed to be like this." She choked back tears. "I don't want to go back there. Not to that apartment."

Jimmy looked at Toddrick. It was a quick look, subtle, but it spoke volumes. I knew Toddrick understood it because he sighed and sat back down.

"Do you have a place to go?" Jimmy asked.

"I'll figure something out." Faye stood and handed the sweater back to him.

He didn't take it. "It's cold outside. You can keep it."

She looked like she was about to refuse, but she thought better of it and slid the hooded sweatshirt over her head. She was so small that it swallowed her like she was a child. She eyed the exit.

"Hang on," Jimmy said. "Let us take you somewhere."

Toddrick dialed a number on his phone. "Give me a second, guys. I think I have a place."

Jimmy stared at Faye. "Listen," he said. "I know this is strange, but I kinda liked beating your boyfriend up."

"He's not my boyfriend," she corrected without

smiling.

Jimmy hemmed. "Wanna grab lunch tomorrow?"

She exhaled. "Look, I gotta figure out what's going on with me before I do anything with anyone."

"All right." Toddrick shoved his phone back in his pocket. "Let's go. I've found a place for you, if you're all right with it."

"I'm not a lost puppy dog that needs a home." She tried to look defiant, but then she retracted. "Thanks. Where?"

"Your neighbor Lisa. She lives below you. She has an extra bed in her room. You can stay there for a few nights while you sort things out. What do you think?"

Faye put her hands over her eyes. "Thanks for asking. I just started a job at Smoking Joe's. I really can't miss my shift tomorrow. It's right next to our apartment complex." She looked like she was considering the offer. "Staying in the same complex would be really convenient."

"Joe's!" Jimmy exclaimed. "I love that place. Of course, I haven't been back there since I was accused of murder."

Faye looked at him skeptically. "Murder, huh?" She looked at Toddrick. "Okay. Thanks. I can grab my stuff from Jay's and bring it to your girlfriend's."

"Fiancé, actually," he corrected.

She smiled despondently. "I hear them talk about me through the ceiling. I'm not a slut."

Toddrick shook his head. "Lisa doesn't think that. She's happy to help. Just work it out with her." He walked toward the door. "Let's get out of here. It's four in the morning, and I'm exhausted."

Faye leaned over and kissed Jimmy on the cheek.

"Thanks again." She smiled. "For helping me with Jay."

"My pleasure," he said.

She looked at him playfully. "Accused of murder how? I should know before I go to lunch with you."

"Yep. I kissed another man's girl, and we fought over it. That night he ended up dead."

"Really? And I thought you were kidding."

CHAPTER THIRTY-FIVE

I went to a lot of weddings. I recall one in particular that was proceeded by such fanfare and extravagance that all invited felt honored to attend. The chapel was adorned with beautiful and costly cloths, tapestries, and flowers. A live band performing romantic songs set the appropriate mood. The appetizers and drinks were divine. Those attending dressed in their finest. So grand was the wedding, the structure, and the beautification of the event that I can't recall whose matrimony it was. But I remember the grandeur of the event. I remember that the bride's wedding gown cost more than my first car. I just can't remember who she was.

A lot of money was poured into the event.

I also attended a wedding that was held in a small and undecorated building. There was no food or wine and no band to play music. The list of guests was not long, nor were those invited counted in high social circles. But I remember the way Aaron and Chrissie, bride and groom, looked at each other as they said their vows. The connection, the love between them was easy to see. They are easy to remember. Always in my mind, in fact.

The difference between the party and the ceremony is an important distinction. One is essential, and one, in the grand scheme of things, is meaningless. As I attended more and more weddings in life, or witnessed them on television, it was obvious to me that something was missing. More and more attention was placed on the event and less and less focus on the binding of husband and wife.

I think there was a time when the love came first and the celebration was secondary. Now there is nothing wrong with a party. Everyone loves a good celebration. But parading love in fancy clothes, feeding it fancy cakes, and displaying it to the masses does not preserve nor enhance the tender feelings that make a relationship endure.

As Toddrick and Lisa planned their own wedding, I watched with peace. No one else mattered. Lisa's simple white dress was beautiful and unadorned. The invitations were few but meaningful. There was so much love and excitement between the two of them that it was impossible for those nearby to question their love.

Amid the good feelings of preparing for a wedding, a new friendship developed between Lisa and Faye. Faye, who had permanently moved in with Lisa, was easy-going and somber. As I watched her interact with Toddrick and Jimmy, I wondered how it was possible that a woman like her could have been with a man like Jay.

How do people become who they are?

I'm going to guess that neither Faye nor Jay ever wanted to become who they'd become. But once you become something, it's hard to be anything else. It took a cataclysmic event for Faye to find the motivation she needed to change.

And change she did.

Jimmy went through a transition of his own. The heartache he'd experienced with Melodee faded to oblivion. The memories of that past love were as one grain of sand on the beaches of the world. Toddrick's and Lisa's positive influence were a soothing balm to his now-distant agony. Like buoys in the water, they were ever ready to lift him up.

And yet, it was Faye who helped Jimmy the most. She developed true feelings for him well before he did for her.Jimmy pursued her because, in his own words, "she was amazingly hot." It was Faye who let the friendship blossom into more than attraction. I suspect that on the first night they met, when she watched Jimmy take down Jay during his tirade, she saw a part of Jimmy that the rest of us hadn't. Loyalty, tenacity and selflessness.

They were similar on so many levels, Faye and Jimmy.

Now I'm going to say something that might get me in trouble, but I'm dead, and the repercussions you can impose upon me are severally limited. I worried about Jimmy being alone with Faye. Not only was she extremely beautiful, but she was equally immodest, and obviously not opposed to intimacy before marriage, something I'd cautioned those two against. Sex is natural, beautiful and normal.

I was relieved that the relationship between Jimmy and Faye developed from that strong physical attraction into a stronger friendship. The dynamics of the relationship were more moderate than Jimmy had experienced with Melodee, but they were sure and true. The light inside Jimmy grew bigger and more luminous then ever before. His smiles and laughter eclipsed that of his former life.

Change. True change.

And so it was that Toddrick and Lisa scheduled their marriage. In a matter of months, they would start their life together as a permanent family.

They would always have ties with their parents and siblings, but the focus of life would become different. Quite unintentionally, and unfortunately for Jimmy, marriage has a way of excluding the single.

Jimmy saw the writing on the wall. He insisted that Toddrick and Lisa would be vacuumed off to some distant oblivion, never to be heard from again except on holidays and family reunions.

They would joke about it sometimes, the strange and indefinable void that swallowed people up after they got married. Friends became acquaintances, and fun became less fun or no fun at all. It was the unspoken phenomena of dividing the available from the unavailable, the attached from the unattached.

There was no escaping it. And *it* was fast on the horizon.

To honor the end of single life, Toddrick and Lisa wanted one final hurrah. They chose a self-navigated, week-long boating trip down the Snake River, a large tributary to the Mississippi. Those two boys, Lisa, and Faye packed camping gear and rented a dark blue rubber raft. They mapped out their route and began to float atop the lazy water.

The water was calm, smooth, and slow. Easy floating made for great conversation, laughs, and pointless observations. They were on nobody's schedule, so meals were long, and both nights and mornings were late. They were relaxed and enjoyed each other's company.

For two days on the water, there wasn't a care in the world. Only mosquitos, catching fish, and making memories. On the third day, the river took a few hard turns south, and the current became stronger and faster. Everyone noticed the change in the water's pace. The real fun was about to begin.

They planned to stop for an early lunch to ensure their gear was packed tightly, just in case the waters became too rough. Up until that point, the gear lying about in the open hadn't been an issue. But the farther they moved down the river, the more the rapids chopped at the water, creating hundreds of white capped waves.

They grounded the raft at the first available spot and broke out supplies to make lunch and prepare for the rapids ahead. Water ran swift around the rocks, and the sound of a million tiny splashes reverberated in the air. The cannonade of noise seemed as loud as Niagara Falls. They shouted at each other to be heard above the liquid cacophony.

"Exciting," Faye said, bumping Jimmy with her shoulder. "The water is super-fast." She spread peanut butter on a piece of bread. "I've never done anything like this before." She pressed the bread together and took a bite from her sandwich.

"I know. This is great," Lisa said. "I'm looking forward to the rapids."

They were eager to get back in the water. Lunch took no time at all. They secured the gear and piled back into the raft. Toddrick and Jimmy grabbed paddles and pushed off the shore.

"I forgot my life jacket," Lisa shouted. She pointed to her blue life vest. It was sitting under the tree where she'd eaten her lunch.

"Hang on," Toddrick shouted. He pointed to a patch of calmer water. "Let's re-dock there and get the vest."

They paddled frantically to get back to shore, but the rapids were stronger than they anticipated. In seconds they were careening down the white-capped water, Lisa still without her life vest.

The first cascade of rocks nearly rocketed Lisa from the raft. Had Toddrick not grabbed her leg, she would have fallen into the water. Toddrick pulled her close, unstrapped his life jacket, and slid it around her shoulders. He buckled it around her chest. "Don't worry," he said, "I'm a really strong swimmer."

"We need to get to shore!" Jimmy yelled. His face betrayed his concern. "It's not safe without a life jacket."

"Well," Toddrick shouted, "let's get to shore, then."

"Guys!" Faye screamed. She pointed down river. "Those are big rocks ahead. Hold on to something!"

Even with Faye's warning, the force of the collision was underestimated. The raft smashed into boulders the size of pickup trucks. It bounced back and forth like a Ping-Pong ball between paddles. The strong current pinned the raft to a large boulder. The upward momentum of the river flipped it over, spilling all the contents. Equipment and people.

Jimmy's head was the first to break the surface of the river. Lisa and Faye emerged next. They bobbed in the water, held afloat by their life jackets. The current sent them all in different directions. The water was spotted with both shallow and deep pockets, great rocks under the water creating platforms in random places. Jimmy found footing and stood. He spotted Faye and Lisa dragging themselves to safety. He scanned the water.

"Where's Toddrick?" Jimmy cupped his hands around his mouth like a cone. "Toddrick!" He yelled for his brother, but the thunderous water swallowed the sound of his voice.

From where he stood, he could see Lisa and Faye nestled safely against the shore. It had been seconds since the raft capsized, but it was too long for Toddrick to be underwater.

Just a few yards away, hands shot out of the water, searching for something to grab. Toddrick's orange helmet was visible for a split second, but then it disappeared beneath the turbulence.

The expression on Jimmy's face said it all. Concern, panic, fear, determination, love. Toddrick's hands above the water meant he was still alive, but if he didn't get air soon he was going to die. He'd been underwater for less than fifteen seconds, but he was obviously struggling against the currents. It was only a matter of time before the oxygen in his system would be wasted.

Jimmy dove in where he'd seen the orange of Toddrick's helmet. The frigid water enveloped him. He forced his eyes to stay open as debris accosted his face. The churning bubbles blocked his view. The current pulled at his feet, but the life jacket wouldn't let him dive deep.

His hands flailed in the murky water, searching for Toddrick. Something knocked his feet. It was too soft to be a rock and felt out of place in the water, there one second then gone the next. He used all his strength to fight against the buoyancy of the preserver that was saving his life. He got down several feet into the water and spotted the orange helmet again. Toddrick was waving his arms and kicking his feet, but then his movement slowed and his body went still.

There was no time to lose. Toddrick was dying or dead, and Jimmy knew if there was any chance to save him, he would have to act now. There wasn't time to go back to the surface and get more air, even though he desperately needed it.

Jimmy unbuckled his life vest, held it in one hand, and disappeared under the water. His hands found his brother's flailing body. With every ounce of strength he had, Jimmy fought the life vest, forcing it under the water. Spots blacked out his vision, and his lungs screamed for air. He secured the life vest around Toddrick's body and let go.

The moment he let go, the water sucked them away from each other.

Toddrick's orange helmet surfaced, followed by his body, wrapped in Jimmy's life vest.

Jimmy didn't come back up.

CHAPTER THIRTY-SIX

Jimmy saved Toddrick, but in so doing lost his own life. For one to live, the other had to die.

By the time Lisa and Faye pulled Toddrick out of the water, he was half-dead. Lisa, who had her CPR certification, had the sense to revive her fiancé. Had she not been capable of that, I would be waiting here for both of my sons.

As it is, I'm just waiting for Jimmy.

So you've listened to their story—the story of those two boys. My sons.

It's taken me a few hours to tell it, and you've been a good listener. If the life story of those two wasn't enough, I'll give you a secret to help ease your mind about life after Earth.

Time.

Yes, *time* is the secret. I've been waiting seconds for Jimmy to come out of the clouds that act as the doorway between earth and immortality. Seconds ago, Jimmy died, and it took me hours to tell you their story. I say hours because that word means something to you, you people waiting to die.

Seconds, minutes, hours, years, decades, centuries, millennia, eons. Just words. Words that mean nothing here. Time has become one big circle, a never ending line that I can walk. Time only exists when you are waiting for something. Here, we only talk about time as it relates to those left on Earth.

You'll see when you get here. Time ends, and eternity opens up.

***

The firmament in front of me rolls back, and a figure breaks through the clouds. He walks toward me. I smile and extend my arms for an embrace.

"Jimmy," I say as I wrap my arms around him. I look him up and down but rest my gaze on his eyes. I can't hold back the smile. "I love you, son." I pull away, not sure how he feels about seeing me.

"I love you too, Dad." Jimmy returns my smile and pats my shoulder. "It's been a long time."

I nod. "It has."

Jimmy looks concerned. "Is Toddrick here?"

I sigh, feigning disappointment. "Unfortunately . . . he isn't." I beam proudly. "You saved him."

"That's a relief," he says. "It would be a shame to go through all that stress and both of us not make it."

"You surprised me, son." I'd gotten used to Toddrick coming to Jimmy's rescue all the time. Toddrick was the one who, time and time again, saved Jimmy. That's how it was. That's how it always had been.

Jimmy looks at me and boasts a handsome grin. "I can't count the number of times Toddrick saved me from something. Usually myself. It's about time I returned the favor."

About the Author

Rheyn D. Maker is a world-traveler who loves noodles most of all. He loves exotic beauty in the form of a black-haired girl who married him and feeds him noodles. He hates headaches and gets them often. But life is pretty good. The end.